HUMPTY'S BONES

HUMPTY'S BONES
SIMON CLARK

First published in the UK in 2010 by
Telos Publishing Ltd
17 Pendre Avenue, Prestatyn, Denbighshire, LL19 9SH
www.telos.co.uk

Telos Publishing Ltd values feedback. Please e-mail us
with any comments you may have about this book to:
feedback@telos.co.uk

ISBN: 978-1-84583-859-1

The author would like to thank James Howe for Latin
translations.

British Library Cataloguing in Publication Data.
A catalogue record for this book is available from the
British Library.

For Janet

HUMPTY'S BONES AND OTHER SKELETAL FRAGMENTS

Introduction

We're in the graveyard. A cold November day. The ancient tower of St Lawrence's Church looms over us. Centuries of burials have raised the ground immediately around the church by four feet or so. The soil is dark; so very, very dark. Meandering amongst the tombs, we read inscriptions: *William Tobias Wrelter, drowned at sea in Scarborough Bay, 1863.* That makes for a salty grave I tell myself. *Kathleen Prior, died in her one hundredth year. After much pain there is peace.* And on the back of one headstone, visible from the road, is engraved a mischievous reminder of our mortality: *Until you follow me: Peace be unto you.*

My daughter, Helen, then aged seven, is interested in a patch of freshly turned soil where someone has planted pansies.

'Cornflakes,' she announces. 'Why has someone left cornflakes in the graveyard?'

'Maybe someone lost their breakfast.'

'Dad!'

Okay, I admit it. The typically bad Dad joke. Usually, finished off with a tickle, or a playful throttle, to distract the child from a lack of parental wit.

Choking with laughter, Helen cries, 'The cornflakes! Where do all the cornflakes come from?'

'Ah ...' Serious now, I examine the disturbed earth. 'They aren't cornflakes, they're pieces of bone.'

'Bone. How did bone get here?'

'It is a graveyard.'

Helen's too smart to be patronised. So I explain that these grey flakes are the bones of our village's ancient dead. The church is built on a pagan temple site, so burials here, of some sort or other, stretch back into prehistory. Nothing dramatic happened to the old tombs as far as I know. Nobody dug up the skeletons and smashed them to pieces in a frenzied orgy of post mortem destruction. Instead, down through the centuries, the old, forgotten burial plots were accidentally recycled in what is, after all, a restricted tract of hallowed ground. Old bones got mixed with the soil-fill. Gradually, these, in some semblance of resurrection, worked their way to the surface to rest in the light of that cold November day.

Helen, being inquisitive, immediately picks them up to examine them. The fragments do resemble cornflakes – although a bony, pale grey in colour. And if you've just eaten cornflake cereal, or are just about to, I apologise for the comparison. So whatever you do, when you spoon those crunchy morsels into your mouth, don't think about crispy fragments of human skull. Remember: cornflakes are nice to eat. Pieces of ancient skeleton – though they resemble cornflakes – are not!

The bygone people of my village buried their deceased relatives in the churchyard. Back then, the proper Christian thing to do, of course. They had no idea that subsequent burials would bring the bones of the beloved to the surface.

And here's the notion that fascinates me, and which neatly nudged me into writing *Humpty's Bones*: whatever we dispose of by burying underground, it has a habit of returning. Which could be a metaphor for the revenant returning to haunt a house. However, it's important to appreciate that whatever we bury is not only likely to creep back to the surface, it also returns in an altered stated. When objects are buried – whether corpses, coins, chemicals, or secret stuff we don't want people to know about – it has this knack of undergoing a transformation.

The cornflake-look-alike skull shards were fleshless after all these centuries. They were also uncannily insubstantial. As if the bone's density had altered, leaving them as light and as crisp as ... well ... flakes of toasted corn. In my garden I found a musket ball; salts in the soil have leeched metal from it, too, so it is peculiarly weightless. A Roman cloak pin made of bronze came to my notice a while ago, poking from a flower bed. Again, the earth had sucked some of the ore from it, leaving it almost porous. These artefacts are ghostly versions of their former selves.

Perhaps the ancients got it right. They often buried their dead in womb-like tombs to prepare the deceased for rebirth. Perhaps some race memory acted on me when I wrote *Humpty's Bones*. I imagined what it would be like to find an ancient burial in a supposedly ordinary garden. Yet it couldn't just be some inert skeleton, could it? Those buried instincts that I (and you) share with our prehistoric ancestors couldn't permit a person's skeleton to be entirely lifeless. Deep down, we suspect that interred bones are merely resting. That they will have a future, and a life of sorts. Yet after so long in the earth an alchemy must have taken place, and they will possess a power to touch our lives in some uncanny way.

So: welcome to my world ... a world where there is a pleasant garden. Near the garden wall there are fruit trees. Concealed in their roots, mysterious bones. One by one they are rising to the surface. Now, push aside that bowl of cornflakes (not that you have an appetite for them anyway now); walk into the garden with me. And we'll recite these words as we go:

Humpty Dumpty sat on a wall,
Humpty Dumpty had a great fall ...

Simon Clark
Yorkshire
4th December, 2009

HUMPTY'S BONES

SIMON CLARK

Humpty Dumpty sat on a wall,
Humpty Dumpty had a great fall.
All the king's horses,
And all the king's men,
Couldn't put Humpty together again.

So, if they can't, who can?

1
Monday Afternoon: 3.03

'The train doesn't want me to go there.'

She'd murmured the words under her breath. Yet an old man in a turban, dozing in a nearby carriage seat, must have thought she'd intended him to hear.

'Then you should go back home.'

Slightly flustered by having the stranger talk to her, Eden Page smiled. 'Pardon?'

'Go home.'

His dark brown eyes regarded hers ... *such wise, old eyes,* she thought. And he sat there with such quiet dignity.

'I can't go home,' she replied. 'It's just not possible.'

'Oh.'

'I wish I could.'

'Then find somewhere else to go. You should always respect omens. If we are sent a warning that we should cease our course of action then we must take heed.' His accent was pure Yorkshire, yet his Asian ancestry gifted him a melodic way of stressing certain words: *Home ... omens ... warning ...* 'I bought a power saw,' he continued. 'It's so hard to cut wood straight without one. My brother borrowed it before I could use it. "Give me it back, it's mine," I told him every time I saw him. He always forgot. This went on for six months. Then I needed the power saw to fit a kitchen worktop. I drove to his house. The car got a puncture. It never stopped raining. My brother wasn't there when I arrived. I had to wait one hour. When I got the saw home I saw the plug had been smashed. I had to fix that first. So frustrating ... so annoying. However! At last I could switch on my expensive power tool and –' He held up his deep brown hand. His first finger ended at the second joint. 'I only went and cut the thing off.' His face remained impassive. 'Blood everywhere. Dripping down the walls. Turned the kitchen sink bright red. Eight hours in hospital. Six stitches. Arm in a sling for a month, so ... If you see omens.' He held up the ruined finger. 'Beware, beware, beware.' He appeared satisfied he'd offered his advice, because he turned to gaze out at the flat landscape that rolled past the carriage window. The train clickety-clacked along the line. A slow heart-beat of a sound.

For a moment Eden wasn't sure whether to thank the man for the advice, or elaborate on why she couldn't go home, or even enquire if his finger still hurt him, but within seconds his eyelids drooped shut as he drifted off to sleep.

The leg space between seats had been judged adequate by a midget. Her knees pressed into the seat in front of her until her toes went numb. The train's temperature had been regulated by someone with the biology of a reptile. From vents hot air beat into her face. To add to her discomfort a promised one hour train ride had turned into more than two. Torrential rain had flooded the tracks overnight, so the machine could only creep along at a dozen miles an hour. Even then it had to slow to a tortoise crawl when it encountered tracks covered with water. On occasions, it seemed as if Eden's train was more boat than land vehicle, as it inched its way through entire lagoons that engulfed these flatlands with a pale brown liquid. It seemed more primeval swamp than ploughed cornfields. The branches of trees clutched at thin air, as if desperately trying to prevent themselves from drowning in all that muddy goo.

Apart from the old man and herself there was only a middle aged couple in the carriage. They sat at the other end and improvised sandwiches from a loaf and packet of crisps. Eden caught sight of her reflection in the glass. Short dark hair framed an uncharacteristic, for her, weary face. Normally her blue eyes twinkled with youthful verve. She worked as a university accommodation officer in Manchester: that required boundless energy to rush up and down stairs at apartment blocks and deal with the students' domestic problems. And at twenty-five years of age that personal vigour was something she was proud of. Eden fought for her students' tenant rights and personal safety like a lioness. When a teenager, living away from home, locked their room door they must feel secure. They had to know that gas heaters wouldn't poison them; nor would light switches electrocute. Eden Page: their untiring guardian. She always delivered – relentless, energetic, dedicated, never saying 'die'. But this journey had turned hellish. The heat inside the carriage drained the strength right out of her.

The train slowly rumbled through unchanging landscape. Dead flat fields divided by overflowing dykes. Intermittent lagoons of murky floodwater. A completely level horizon that amputated cool green-brown earth from a darkening sky. *The train doesn't want me to go there.* The notion came back to haunt her along with the man's words. *'You should always respect omens … beware, beware, beware …'*

Eden opened her eyes with a start. Everyone in the carriage had gone. She must have fallen asleep soon after the conversation with the man across the aisle, not even noticing when the train had pulled into stations.

The machine trundled across the same monotonous landscape. Fields, flooded dykes. No houses, no trees to speak of. *Have I missed my stop?* The threat of having to ride the train back the way she'd already painfully come brought her fully awake. *Where's the conductor? I'll feel such an idiot for having to ask if I've missed the station. And how long will it take to get back? Probably hours, considering the speed of this train. It's almost at a standstill.*

She rubbed gritty eyes. The heat had dried her lips to the point they felt shrivelled. The train's crawl became a groaning inch-by-inch judder. Then, at long, long last, a platform appeared alongside her. Painfully, the train oozed into a desolate looking station. She read the heavily weathered sign. *Dog Lands. At last … at long suffering last …*

Eden Page hefted her over-stuffed hold-all out through the carriage doors onto the wet platform. It still hadn't quite stopped raining. Heavy drops tapped the top of her head like the flick of a finger. As the train groaned its way out of the station into the embrace of endless farmland, she plonked the bag onto a bench, then tugged her phone from her coat pocket. Eden had last been here as a child. It hadn't changed much. The

unmanned station, consisting of a pair of barren
platforms, stood between fields of potatoes. A lane
connected it with the main road about two hundred
yards away. Another hundred yards along that stood the
village of Dog Lands. Even when she was a girl the name
Dog Lands had seemed peculiar. A peculiarity that
extended to the village, too. Often, old English villages
nestle in valleys, or shelter in a snug swathe of trees. The
houses of Dog Lands stood proud of the flat Yorkshire
landscape as if striving hard not to be part of it, like
family members trying to distance themselves from that
troublesome, eccentric uncle at a wedding. Once, as a ten
year old, she'd counted the houses when she waited with
her mother for the train. 'Look, Mum, there are thirteen
houses,' she'd declared brightly.

As she waited for the phone to find a signal, she
counted the box-shaped houses again, and once more
she found herself whispering, 'Look, Mum, there are
thirteen houses.' A tongue-in-cheek homage to the quiet,
bookish child she once was. She took a deep breath.
After the heat of the train at least she found Dog Lands
coolly refreshing.

Eventually, she had bars on her phone screen.
Eden tried making the call five times straight. Each time,
after ten rings, she only reached voicemail. 'Oh come on
… you promised.' A gust of wind brought a rattle of
raindrops against the platform. She thumbed the call
button again. 'Be in, be in,' she urged under her breath.
'Please be in.' After five minutes of trying she decided to
walk. Even though it had been many years since her last
visit here she remembered the shortcut path to her aunt's
house. It ran on where the station's access lane ended.
So, after hauling the hold-all strap over one shoulder,
she exited the platform for the half mile trudge to the

house, which lay in the other direction, standing well apart from the village. Even in this grey gloom of a damp spring afternoon she could make out its hard cube shape standing tall on the open landscape.

Eden had barely covered the first hundred yards of the path when she realised it would be tough going. Her route followed a narrow canal between yet more featureless fields. The path consisted of nothing more than compacted red shale that had turned into a rust-coloured glue that tried to stick her feet to it as she trudged, slopped, slithered along. There was no-one else in sight. No vehicles. Square fields either pushed potato, sugar beet or turnip out of their moist, earthen bodies. In one field, a solitary cow watched her walk by. Clearly it didn't like what it saw, because it lumbered in the other direction. As she plodded the slimy track she used the phone again only to be rewarded by her aunt's invitation to leave a message at the tone.

The path got worse. Pools of water extended over it. Eden had to either make giant, gusset-wrenching strides, or tip-toe along the edge where the water didn't reach. By the time the path ran through a clump of bushes it had assumed the guise of a stream. As she picked her way forward, her jaw set in a determined way, she heard an animal growl. Clearly a dog, but an unseen dog. A breeze gave the bushes a shake, making them hiss loudly. The dog snarled again. Eden stooped a little to see if it lay under the branches. Hardly any light made it through the foliage; the area beneath the bushes lay in deep gloom. No dog. At least none she could see. She leapt to a bump in the ground that formed a tiny island. The dog growled loudly. A rumbling note of warning. 'Great,' she murmured, 'the cow turned its back on me – now the local dogs have taken exception to me.' She repositioned the hold-all strap across her shoulder. 'But you're not going to turn me back. I'm going forward.'

She managed a step in the right direction. One that would take her along the only shortcut to her aunt's home. However, that single step brought another growl from the undergrowth. This changed in tone. The first growls had been the 'mouth closed' kind of muted growl, this had become a 'jaws open' snarl. She pictured an upper canine lip curling back to expose gleaming fangs. Another step along her chosen path brought a louder snarl, with an even greater emphasis on the warning note.

A feral dog? It's possible in a place like this. But I'm not going to walk the long way round. I'm pushing on. A sudden movement in the shadows made her jump. 'Damn.' Immediately she felt a stab of annoyance at the way she'd flinched. *I'm not the timid sort. I bite back.* The snarls grew more menacing with every step she took. And still she hadn't seen so much as a canine ear or a pooch whisker. *What if it's a bitch with a new litter of puppies under there? She'd only be protecting her babies.* Eden recalled the way she upbraided landlords for renting rooms to students that had windows repaired with cardboard, or were so damp that fungus grew on bedroom walls. The notion of a bitch protecting vulnerable newborns made her pause. She felt a pang in her stomach that was a sense of affinity. *If I disturb the mother then she might abandon her puppies. Or am I finding a reason for not going on – and for not admitting I'm scared?*

Another loud snarl erupted from the bushes – most definitely the open mouth kind, with sharp teeth savagely glinting no doubt (although Eden hadn't so much as glimpsed the animal). 'Okay, okay, you win,' she breathed. A moment later, she retraced her steps. 'I suppose I have to take the long way to the house,' she told herself with a sigh. On passing the station she noticed the sign again. 'Dog Lands. After being turned back by a bad-tempered mutt, don't you love the irony?' She shook her head. 'And the name of the house where you will be staying? Now, what do they call that, Miss Eden Page?' A grim smile tugged her mouth. 'Why, Miss Page, they call that house Dog Star.' She hefted the heavy bag as its strap bit into her shoulder. 'Dog Lands. Dog Star. A wild dog. It doesn't get any better than this, does it?' From those words, uttered half-humorously, to knowing that she had to take the longer road route to Dog Star House was only a hop and a skip to recollecting what the man on the train had said. *'You should always respect omens ... beware, beware, beware ...'* Eden was normally so level-headed and rational, yet all of a sudden the man's words had all the resonance of a warning. One directed at her intention to throw herself on the mercy of a family member she hadn't met in years.

2

Monday Afternoon: 5.45

Eden Page found her aunt. She was at the bottom of her garden, and under a large gazebo. Why she stood shoulder-deep in a hole beneath an awning in the rain, and why she picked lumps of mud from that chasm Eden didn't know or care. The walk from the station had been punishing. The road that pierced the village was dead straight and encouraged vehicles to speed dangerously. Passing farm trucks had splashed her. The hold-all's dead weight hurt her shoulder, she was sure a whopper of a bruise was blooming there from her skin.

'Heather! You were supposed to collect me from the station. You promised!' Eden threw the hold-all down onto the grass. 'I kept calling! Why didn't you answer the phone?'

'Eden! Watch where you're putting your feet. Those are fragile. I've just spent the last two hours getting them out in one piece.'

'What?'

'Move back from there. Further back. No, to your left. Oh! You've trod on one. Whatever you do, don't do

23

any more damage! No, stand still. Stop tramping round like a – oh!' Heather slapped her hand down onto the rim of the pit in which she stood. 'Eden! You stood on the tile, you –'

Idiot girl? Don't ever call me 'you idiot girl' again!

Her aunt finished the sentence, however with, 'you'll break the only complete tile I've found.'

Eden hadn't seen her aunt in almost a decade. Back then, the woman hadn't been slow to address her with that scathing, 'you idiot girl'. Now events had moved on. Eighteen months ago, her aunt, Heather Laird, had inherited Dog Star House from her mother. Heather was an accountant; her only child served in the Merchant Navy; at fifty-three she possessed the same youthful vigour as the Page side of the family. Right at that moment Heather (always 'Heather' to Eden – never 'Aunt') stood in a hole up to her shoulders. Above her stood a portable gazebo shelter of the type that can be bought in garden centres. Raindrops hung and dripped from the sides in slow procession.

Grimly suggestive, the oblong slit in the earth in which Heather stood resembled an open grave. Heather's body possessed a wiry toughness, her hair had been scraped back tight into a pony tail. Her hands were thick with dirt right up to the elbows. As Eden stood there glaring, Heather reached down into the hole and hoisted out a boulder the size of a water melon. The muscles in her arms protruded from her skin with perfect definition. Handling the rock confidently, she rolled it across the rough grass away from the pit's side

Eden wasn't for one moment going to let talk of cracked tiles brush aside her complaint. 'Heather. Why didn't you pick me up from the station? I've had to walk for the best part of an hour. I'm soaked.'

Heather cried out. 'Ah! Here's another one! My God, not just one ... I don't believe it. One, two, three, four. There must be another dozen. Here, hold out your hand. I'll give you one at a time. Careful, careful! Put them in the plastic tray over there by the chair. Not the white tray, the green one. Gently, don't drop it in. Do you see? Green tray for coins, white for potsherds. The big red bowl's for bones.'

Eden looked from what appeared to be a small pebble that Heather had placed in her open hand to where the woman stood in the grave-shaped pit. A battery-powered lamp lit the bottom of it brilliantly. It was as if Heather stood in a bath of silver radiance. Rich, brown walls of earth gave way to a black floor littered with lumps of stone the size of shoe boxes. The rich soil odours were almost intoxicating.

Heather crouched to scrape dirt with a trowel. 'I can't wait for the rain to stop so I put this up.' She pointed up at the canvas awning with her trowel. 'The work must go on.'

'Work? You mean this hole?'

'Excavation. I've found the remains of a Roman outbuilding; the actual villa is over in that field; alas, the villa's discovery is nothing to do with me – it was uncovered by the county archaeological unit a couple of years ago. Naturally I'm not allowed to touch that. English Heritage whacked it with a preservation order. If I so much as look at it I'll be sued. But this is my land, so this is my Roman tool-shed, or stable, or whatever it is. I've spent the last three weeks excavating. And no bloody rain's going to stop me.'

'Or picking your niece up from the station?'

'Sorry about that.' Heather briefly glanced up as she scraped crumbs of earth from the bottom of the pit. 'I only hope this damp won't make the sides collapse.'

'You said if I phoned from the station that you or Curtis would –'

'Yippee, another one. Heavy. At least three fused together. Big – could be early sestertii.'

'Heather! I had to walk an hour ... in the rain ... with that bag. You don't –'

'I said I'm sorry.' Heather's eyes flicked from the fused lump of coins to Eden standing above her. 'But you didn't confirm what day you were arriving. I thought it was tomorrow.'

'I said all along, Monday.'

'Well, never mind. The main thing is you're here, safe and sound. Nice to see you again, by the way, after all these years. Do the honours, will you?' She handed Eden the coins glued together by decay. 'Make yourself useful. Green tray, remember.'

Eden sighed, realising that there was no point in pursuing a heartfelt expression of regret from her aunt. She laid the green-brown lump in the tray alongside the other grimy objects.

'So these really are coins?'

'They are. Masses of them. A real hoard. Isn't it fantastic!' Heather spoke with gusto. 'And all at the bottom of my garden.'

'Valuable?'

'I've winkled out about five hundred Roman so far, all bronze. In that uncleaned state I might be lucky to get fifty pounds for them. If I spend six months brushing them, soaking them in olive oil, brushing again and again and again – always careful to preserve the patina – I might get three hundred quid. It's hardly worth the effort, is it?' She wiped her brow. Some of the dirt from her hand painted a dark streak across her forehead. 'It's not the cash, it's what I can learn about the Roman settlement here that's so interesting.' Her eyes shone. 'No. More than interesting. Fascinating!'

Eden looked at the state of Heather. 'You're not afraid to get your hands dirty.'

'What, this? Best antique earth there is. And it soon washes off. Listen, Eden, I'll make it up to you later. Have a hot shower. A change of clothes, then plenty of Curtis's pizza – and loads and loads of ice-cold wine.' She continued to rattle the words at high velocity, hardly pausing for breath. 'So far I've found a brooch, a leather loop, you wouldn't believe it, leather is eternal; I found a Roman shoe complete with hobnails. All this because we decided to plant apple trees at the bottom of the garden. Just under the turf I found twentieth century pennies, sixpences, shillings. The deeper I got the older the coins got. Edwardian. Victorian. Eighteenth century – you should see some of those whoppers; there are pennies the size of jar lids. I kept digging, the coins kept coming. Medieval groats, tenth century Norman then all the way back nearly two thousand years. Right back to when this country was part of the Roman empire and chariots would be zipping along that road across there. That's Roman too, of course, the *Via Britannicus*. Here. Look at this. You'll find this interesting.' She wiped her muddy hand on her shirt and then delved into her jeans pocket to draw out a little plastic envelope, which she handed to Eden. 'See that? A sestertius of Claudius Gothicus. Great name, eh? It's the best example I've got. See the emperor's profile? The chin shaped like a cake slice? He claimed to be a descendent of Zeus.'

'The coin's not even round. It's more like a half moon.'

'Deliberately broken to make it worthless. In

ancient cultures they believed if you made something on Earth a counterpart came into existence in heaven. Breaking a pot on Earth left the heavenly counterpart intact. Same with coins; this one is chopped in half by a sword or whatever, but the exact twin in heaven is still in one piece. It's a bit hard to explain, but folk in ancient cultures often transferred the value in an object to the gods by destroying it on Earth – burning, chucking in a river, sacrifice.'

Eden could see that the excavation exerted a formidable grip on her aunt. The woman's grey eyes danced with joy when she enthused about the coins.

'Shouldn't you report buried treasure to the authorities?'

'Buried gold and silver, yes. These bronze coins don't have much monetary value. All the pots are broken and even the bones are all burned. But this has really grabbed my imagination. At night I dream that I'm in this hole digging out wonderful objects.'

Heather ducked down into the hole again as she talked, scraping and worrying at something with her trowel. There was a moment's silence. Then she stood again, eyes shining. 'Eden, be an angel and pass me the red bowl.'

'The one with the bones?'

'That's the one. It's obvious now. I don't know why it didn't occur to me before.' She gently pulled out a bone that was as slender and as cylindrical as a water pipe that feeds a domestic sink. Where the mud had flaked off it revealed a smooth black surface. 'Thigh. Like I said, burnt. But not cremated.'

'Oh no.' Eden grimaced. 'You're not saying that these are ...' She deliberately ditched the concluding word.

'Oh, yes, human, I'm sure they're human.' She stared down into the pit. 'That means this is –'

'Heather? Heather!'

'Ah,' Heather sighed, placing the bone carefully in the red bowl. 'Time for you to meet the husband.'

A man in a cream linen suit, his long silver hair tied into a pony tail, bounced along the path. Eden could tell he blazed with so much energy he was an ideal partner for the equally vigorous Aunt Heather. He didn't so much speak into the phone he carried as fire words into it with explosive force.

Heather patted the top of Eden's foot, the only part of her niece she could reach from a pit that was becoming increasingly redolent of a tomb. 'Don't let his manner bother you. His bark his worse than his, you know …'

'I'm sure I'll be fine. Besides, I had an encounter with a ferocious dog earlier. It wouldn't let me walk along the path that runs up to the back wall across there.'

'So that's why you walked the long way round? Eden, you should have told me that a dog had frightened you.'

'Not frightened –'

'It must have given you a scare. Give me your hand.' Before extending hers Heather rubbed her palms on the legs of her jeans to remove some of the dirt. 'Thanks.' With Eden's help she athletically scrambled out of the hole. 'Where was this dog? What did it look like? If it's one of those great things from Hezzle Farm I'll bring the police down on them again, bloody pests.'

'No, don't worry. Besides, I never saw the dog. It kind of …' She shrugged. '… lurked in the bushes.'

'But it must have terrified you, poor thing. Curtis?' Her husband marched across the lawn, still speaking with formidable energy into the phone.

'Curtis. Come off that thing. There's dog trouble again. Eden here, she's been terrified out of her wits.'

Eden felt awkward. 'No, really. It wasn't as frightening as –'

'Curtis?' Heather pressed on. 'Leave that while later.'

Curtis signalled 'one minute'. His brisk, professional tones were at odds with the bohemian hair-style that could have carried the caption: LOOK AT ME. DEEPLY UNCONVENTIONAL, BUT THOROUGHLY BUSINESS-LIKE. SO WATCH YOUR STEP! 'Klein can't have the studio tomorrow. No, I don't care if Wayne gave a verbal assurance that he could. All bookings must be in writing with an upfront deposit. I've got the Dutch band in all week with a weekend option. That's right. They're paying in full for studio time on Saturday whether they want it or not. One's got some big birthday hosanna on Saturday night in Amsterdam. If I pull them out tomorrow, so Klein can noodle around adding pops and squeaks to his computer games, they'll end up having to record through the weekend, and miss the party … they've shelled a lot for the studio, Ben, I'm not going to frick them around. Yeah, well, tell Wayne to say NO to Klein. If he's too much wind and water to do that then kick him out. I'm having no light-weights in the company. And if you won't read the riot act to Wayne … yeah, okay, see that you do.'

Heather must have noticed the expression on Eden's face. 'Told you about the barking, didn't I?' She picked up the plastic bowl to examine the bones. 'Tibia, rib, skull – but that's not right … look at the skull fragment.'

Her husband barked out a louder 'NO! No

preferential rates! Klein pays full! Especially after last time. The place was a pig-sty. I found a vodka bottle in the toilet bowl.'

Under her breath, Heather said, 'Curtis opened a recording studio in York early this year. We still have,' she raised her eyebrows, 'teething troubles. You wouldn't believe the number of people who book studio time then never turn up. Last week the studio's loo flooded. Crap all over the new carpets. Curtis ignited. I've never seen him so angry.' This seemed to remind her. 'Curtis. We've a guest.'

'Heather, just one moment!'

Heather shrugged, then said to Eden, 'Look at the fragment of skull.'

'Human?' Eden made a point of not touching it, even though Heather offered it to her.

'No.' She sniffed. 'Odd. No human fragments of skull. This is dog.

3
Monday Evening: 7.11

In the living room, Curtis poured three glasses of white wine. 'Eden, I'm sorry to hear about your apartment. Were all the rooms affected?'

'There's smoke damage to the living room and the bedroom; they need repainting. Worst is the kitchen. The fire ruined the cupboards and even part of the floor burned through.'

'Good heavens. But the insurance will take care of it?' Even though Curtis had changed into a smock-top and jeans, which could best be described as rural hippy, he still sounded like the no-nonsense business man. Eden decided that many people Curtis met would be surprised by how his bohemian, easy-going appearance was at odds with the waspish manner.

'I'm covered, so they'll pay for the repairs in full. The trouble is the time it'll take. It's been nearly impossible to find a builder, they're all so busy these days. I finally managed to get someone who can start at the end of the month.'

'Long job?'

'Two weeks to get it liveable again.' There was something about Curtis's expression that prompted her to add quickly, 'Are you sure it's alright for me to stay with you for so long?'

'Fine ... its fine.'

'It really is good of you to put me up.'

'No, the pleasure's all ours.' The smile was a tad professional, his eyes cold looking. 'Heather could do with some company. We're isolated out here ... we love the peace of course. And that landscape, once you get use to the flatness, is really quite beautiful you know. Vast open spaces, enormous skies. You can almost reach out and touch the tranquillity of it all.'

Eden found she could only repeat her gratitude. 'Thanks for inviting me to share it with you. I'll do what I can to help out around the house.'

'That's very generous. With Heather standing in that damn hole in the garden all day sometimes the more mundane day-to-day stuff slips. And she has her accountancy work, too.' He laughed. 'We don't want her clients banging on the door, do we? Howling about delayed tax returns. Now ... seeing as Heather won't come out of her lab and leave those bloody bones alone. Shall we take these to her?'

Eden picked up two wine glasses. Curtis followed with his.

'Right to end of the passageway, Eden. Last door on your left. Duck your head; it's the oldest part of the house. The doorways were built for goblins.'

The door was part open, so even with a glass in each hand, Eden managed by pushing it ajar with her elbow. Heather leaned over the long table in the centre of the room, with the kind of expression of concentration someone might wear when immersed in a jigsaw puzzle.

On the table were laid fragments of bone; most still coated with mud. The low-ceilinged room accommodated 'treasures' from the dig: plastic trays full of those greenish copper coins, fragments of pottery, pieces of tile. On a desk in the corner, a microscope and a laptop sat side by side. Heather was oblivious to the new arrivals.

'Have you put the chap back together again, yet?' boomed Curtis.

Heather flinched. She shot him a glare that clearly said, *Don't you dare interrupt me like that!* With Eden being there, Heather managed a polite. 'Oh, you've come to see if I've made any progress? Eden, welcome to the lab, by the way.'

'Lab?' Curtis chuckled. 'This is where they used to do the laundry way back when. So? Humpty Dumpty here ... a Roman Legionnaire stabbed in the vitals, or a Vestal Virgin done horribly to death for being a tease?'

'Ooh, wine. Lovely, thank you.' Heather took the glass, her fingers still coated in good Yorkshire earth. 'And at least it's not too dry.'

'White wine can never be too dry.' As he sipped his he pulled a face that suggested he thought the wine mediocre. 'Please note, Eden, your aunt isn't afraid to get her hands dirty. I tell her that stuff sticking to her fingers ... if what she's digging up is a stable ... is two thousand year old poop.'

'Hardly a stable. The dimensions are too small.'

'A lavatory then. With contents thereof in situ.'

'And these bones. There is definite charring.'

Heather offered a thighbone for her husband to examine more closely. He responded with a terse, 'I'll stay with the *vin blanc*, thank you.' Then: 'Eden was telling me about the fire damage to her apartment.

Terrible state of affairs, isn't it?'

Again Eden felt as if she had to reassure them that her visit wouldn't be a long one. 'And thanks again, Heather for inviting me to stay. I've told Curtis that I'm more than willing to help out around the house; I won't get under your feet.'

Heather gulped her wine. 'A boy, wasn't it? Didn't he do it deliberately?'

Eden tightened her grip on the glass. 'I invited a friend home.'

'But it turned out he didn't give you his real name, did he?' Heather's gaze became uncomfortably penetrating as she regarded Eden.

'That's right. For whatever reason he didn't want to ...' Simply voicing the events that led to the destruction of half her home weren't only painful, but they made her feel so foolish.

Curtis uhmed. 'And you'd only met him the once, I understand?'

'Yes. I feel such an idiot.'

Heather turned back to her bones. 'You're a very trusting person. Your mother's like that. The trouble is that people aren't always nice.'

Curtis took the empty glass from Heather as she picked up a jaw bone; it still had brown canines embedded in the sockets. Almost as if he couldn't stop himself, he added, 'The police think it was arson, don't they?'

Heather murmured, 'You can't be too careful who you let into your home these days.'

'Drug addict, was he? Or insane? Did he look right to you when you met him in the pub?'

Eden's face burned. 'He looked perfectly normal. There was nothing odd about him.'

'Outwardly, maybe. But, with hindsight, you must remember some strange quirk about his behaviour?'

Eden's hand shook enough for a drop of wine to spring over the rim to fall onto the bones laid on the table.

'Careful!' Heather used a tissue to dab wine from a rib bone.

Curtis laughed. 'Did he spend the evening fiddling with a cigarette lighter?'

'Look, I'd had a drink, I was lonely –'

'Eden, there goes more wine. Stand back from the table – *please*.'

Curtis still laughed. 'But a dirty, great keg of diesel would have been a dead giveaway. I wonder what turns people into arsonists?'

'I'm sorry.' Eden's eyes pricked. 'I don't want to talk about it. People could have died that night. My neighbours have children –'

'Uh, there it goes again.' The phone in the passageway began to ring. 'Excuse me.' Curtis vanished back through the door. A second later Eden heard his brisk voice dealing with what appeared to be more problems. 'You've tackled Klein, I hope? He gets no more studio time unless he pays at least half upfront … what's that? If it's not Klein, what is it then? The heating? What do you expect me to do about it this time of night? No, don't call out the engineer. We can't afford to run up more bills. The studio's supposed to generate income for us. At this rate we'll be pouring more cash in than we're getting out. Damn it, Wayne. Look at the thermostat. Somebody's probably just dicked around with the thing. Turn it down; don't expect me to hold your hand while you do it.'

As Curtis fought his battles by phone Heather

murmured, 'Tibia, ribs, though not quite a full set. Vertebrae. Shins. Part of a pelvis. Do you know what we've got here?'

'What?' Eden had been so wound up by this couple's insensitivity that she'd not been listening. If anything, she found herself thinking about her apartment. The stench of smoke that clung to everything. The heat in the kitchen had melted the windows so they hung down the wall like surreal icicles. The mess, the bloody awful, stinking mess.

'Eden, do you know what we've got here?'

'I don't care.'

'Pardon?'

'I'm sorry that my mother asked you to put me up. It's not working out. In the morning I'll –'

'Oh, don't let Curtis bother you. It's just his way. Ever since he set up this studio he's been like an old dog with a sore backside. Growl, growl, growl … I don't even listen to what he says half the time. Water off a duck's back. Now, see this ankle joint. Hardly any wear.'

Eden stared in disbelief. How can anyone take part in what had been a bullying interrogation, then switch subjects like nothing had happened?

Heather pressed on, clearly fascinated by the skeleton. Eden could smell the wet soil. It added to the oppressive air of the house. She longed to go out into the fields and walk and walk until sheer exhaustion released the emotional pressure she felt building inside of her. Heather purred her observations as she lovingly touched each bone in turn. 'No sign of disease, or wear, certainly no arthritis in the big ball joints of the hips. We're looking at the skeleton of a youth, I'm sure of it. Late teens at the most. From the lightness of the bones I'd say he was slightly built. Almost willowy you could say.

Eden? We've been thugs, haven't we? You come here as our guest and we've talked about that fire like it was nothing more than broken plate. You must have been devastated, poor thing.'

'It's not fair!'

'Of course, it isn't. The boy who started the fire must have been psychotic.'

'No, I meant –'

'Wait here. Time for more medicine.'

'No, I meant you've *not been fair.'* But Heather had already vanished through the low doorway and so didn't hear. Meanwhile, in the passage, Curtis loudly reminded the luckless Wayne that all studio bookings required a deposit.

'Poor Wayne,' Eden breathed. 'Poor me.'

For some reason, Heather was delayed long enough for Eden's temper to cool. By the time Heather returned with two more bottles of wine, Eden had begun to take an interest in the trays of coins. One about the size of her thumbnail revealed a human figure through the corrosion.

'That's one of the better preserved ones.' Heather filled Eden's glass. 'Medicine. Drink up.'

'I can make out a man; although it's faint. Almost a ghost.'

'If he's wearing clothes it will be an emperor, if he's nude it will probably be a god. Roman gods loved to disrobe.'

'It's impossible to tell. It's so worn.'

'It'll have gone through a lot of Romano-British hands, no doubt buying flagons of ale. The money might have even belonged to Humpty here.'

'Humpty?' For the first time in a while Eden smiled.

'We have to call this mess of bones something. Humpty Dumpty makes sense. At least until I've put him back together again.' She perused the bones. 'But I'm missing a skull. I have almost a complete human skeleton, but no skull.'

'Only the coins can't be his.'

'Hmm?' Thoughtful, Heather laid neck vertebrae in a line extending from the collar bone.

'The coins. I mean they can't all be his, can they?'

'What makes you think that?'

'Humpty's bones were found *beneath* the coins. You said some are twentieth century.'

'Of course, you're right. Yes, absolutely – some date from the 1990s.'

'So, why have generations of people dropped coins into that exact spot at the bottom of your garden?'

Heather scratched her nose with a dirt crusted finger. 'There was a circular depression there; something like a bomb crater, but only about so big.' She held out her hands to indicate a yard across. 'It did look peculiar, though. It was quite deep. At the time I thought that it might be where a tree had been taken out and the root had pulled out a big chunk of soil. At the bottom of the crater was a hole. I assumed a rabbit had dug it.'

'That's where people had been dropping in coins through the centuries.'

Heather pursed her lips as she thought about it. 'I guess you're right. Perhaps it was the equivalent of a wishing well. You know, toss in a penny and make a wish. So, Humpty.' She addressed the skeleton. 'You've been lying there while folk chucked money at you. Hardly resting in peace, is it?'

'Or they were paying him?'

'Come again?'

Eden nodded at the bones that so much resembled dirty twigs. 'Paying him. Making offerings of coins.'

'Paying him to do what?'

'Stay where he is. Not to harm them.'

Heather stared for a moment, then gave sharp-sounding laugh. 'That's beautifully imagined, Eden.'

'Don't laugh. It's possible.'

'You mean for the last eighteen hundred years men, women and children have been creeping furtively up to the hole and dropping their hard cash into it before scurrying away again before a bony hand darts out to grab them by the ankle?'

'I'm serious, it adds up.'

'Now you're pulling my leg, Eden. Here let me top you up. Is that the time? I must switch the oven on.'

'I've beaten you to it.' Curtis stooped to enter through the low door. 'The pizzas are already in.'

'Is Wayne coping at the studio?'

'The bloody fool. He didn't realise that all he needed to do was to turn down the thermostat to lower the heating. He's had the Dutch band cooking in the control room as they've worked on a sound mix. If Wayne screws up one more time ...' He helped himself to wine. 'Stick with your work, Eden. It's got to be less stressful than running a recording studio. Ah, your bony wee chap has got a neck now.'

Eden said, 'He's also got a name – Humpty.'

'Yes. Humpty Dumpty. What happened to his head?'

'Ah, that's the mystery,' Heather sighed. 'I've nearly a complete skeleton, as far as I can judge.'

'Only no noodle bone?'

Eden made a point of joining in (to ensure talk didn't drift back to the arson), 'No human skull, although Heather's found a dog's jawbone.'

'And parts of the cranium along with an eye ridge.'

'It doesn't surprise me. They're crazy about dogs round here. They even called the village Dog Lands. We're in Dog Star House, and there's all kinds of Dog Lanes, Hounds Heaths. Plus there's a weird carving of a dog in the lintel above the church door. The whole place must be barking mad.'

His wife tutted. 'Wait until I've got more wine inside of me before you go cracking jokes like that.' She took a hefty swallow. 'Hmm. Before I forget: Eden has a theory about the coins.'

'Why there are so many of them? And from different centuries. I must admit that's a strange one.'

'Eden thinks ...' A little smile played on Heather's lips. 'People put money in the hole where the bones were to appease Humpty's ghost.'

'No, I didn't say that.' Eden flushed.

'As near as. You thought they were offerings.'

Curtis chuckled. 'Did you hear that, Humpty?' He crouched down to look at the bones at eye-level. 'If you stay there like a good skeleton I'll bring you a slice of pizza later. What do you say, old chum?'

'Eden –' Heather began.

But Eden had already left the room. *They think I'm a fool,* she thought angrily. *They as good as tell me that I was stupid to bring home an arsonist for a one night stand. Now I've tried to show an interest in Heather's bloody bones they're making fun of me.*

In the gloomy passageway she mistook one door for the way back to the living room. She miscalculated the height of the entrance; a second later Eden smacked her forehead hard against the low lintel.

4
Monday Night: 10.00

'Eden, how's the head now?'

   'Curtis! Just a minute. I'm getting changed.'

   'Sorry. I should have knocked.'

Eden slipped a nightdress over herself. It was a short one so she picked up a towel from the bed. She folded it over her arm as if about to visit the bathroom. At least the way it hung down covered the bareness of her thighs.

   'My head's fine. Come in, if you want.'

   'I'm here too, Eden.' Her aunt stepped through the bedroom door with her husband remaining in the doorway.

   'Are you sure I can't get you anything for your head? That was quite a bang, you know?'

   'An early night will be the best thing for me. It's been a long day.'

   'I expect so.' Curtis nodded. 'You're probably still in shock over that lunatic burning your kitchen. It can't be any fun being made homeless.'

   'It isn't.' Oh no, Eden though. Here we go again. The

third degree. Silly Eden Page falling for a fire-starter. 'I still feel washed out.'

'Surely the police checked for fingerprints and DNA evidence? They say –'

'Curtis,' Heather interrupted. 'Pour the wine. I'll be down in a minute.'

He gave a little shrug as if to say, *Suit yourself. I was only being helpful.* A moment later Eden heard the sound of his footsteps heading downstairs.

'Eden. You will tell me if you need anything, won't you? Remember, if you want a drink at anytime help yourself. Or anything to eat. Don't feel as if you have to ask. We're going to look after you while you're here. You can trust us. Okay?'

'Okay.'

'There's the television. The clock radio is on the washstand. Your bathroom is across the corridor. But for heaven's sake remember to duck your bloody head.' She smiled. 'You know, this is my favourite room. It used to be mine when I was a girl. Do you remember when you stayed here? You used to sleep on the sofa in the room my mother called the snug.'

'Things went bump in the night.' Eden smiled, too. 'I thought there were ghosts.'

'Dodgy plumbing, more like. When I inherited … ooh, eighteen months ago … I had the whole lot ripped out. And those old iron baths, too, that used to freeze your backside in winter.' Heather folded her arms as she casually walked across the room to the window. 'All this is antique furniture. The bed's over a hundred years old but it's all very comfortable. Did your mother feel cheated, because she didn't inherit a share in the house?'

'Pardon?'

'After all, we're sisters. Same mother, if different

father. Not that it matters of course. It doesn't matter one little bit. But your grandmother wanted this house to come to me.'

'Mother's never complained.'

'No, she wouldn't. Daisy – your mother – is a free spirit. Just like you.' Heather studied Eden's face. 'Worldly possessions were never her priority. She was happy in a tent in Glastonbury, living on farm cider and copious love.' Heather must have expected Eden to respond to that rather judgmental statement. When Eden said nothing, however, Heather continued briskly, 'Even though the house was left solely to me I wasn't comfortable about being singled out for preferential treatment by our mother.'

'All Mum did say to me was that she wouldn't contest the will.'

'Even so ...' She pulled aside the curtain. Outside was perfectly black. 'See? We don't even have streetlights here. Maybe there should be one at the bend in the road. Now that bend is rare. The Romans never permitted themselves bends in their roads if they could help it. When they built this road eighteen hundred years ago it ran straight as a laser for ten miles across country. It turns a sharp right at the house, then it turns left to pick up the straight line. That always bothered me.'

'Maybe there was something built here?'

'It would have to be important – very important. Roman highway engineers swept all before them – forests, houses, whole villages if necessary. For them the straight line was divinity itself. At least when it came to roads.'

'Then whatever was built here, on the site of the house, must have mattered to them a lot.' Eden suspected this sudden talk of the road had been to change the subject. But her aunt must have been nagged by the notion of unfinished business.

'The *Via Britannicus* was one of the most important roads in Romano Britain.' She nodded to her left. 'That way, York.' Then right. 'That way ... Rome. Heart of Empire. Favoured city of the gods.' She let the curtain slip back to keep the night at bay. 'I don't know if your mother told you, but when I inherited this place I sent her a cheque. I didn't have to.

'That's entirely her business.'

'In any case, it will have bought a lot of cider and exciting times at music festivals.'

'She won't have wasted the money.'

'I don't suppose she thought she was *wasting* it. Daisy's happy-go-lucky. She will be until the day she dies.'

'Heather. I'm very tired.'

She took the hint. 'We tend to rise early, but you get up when you want. Don't think there are any pressures on you here. We'll keep you safe.'

5
Monday: Midnight

It may have been the chimes of the clock downstairs, striking twelve, that first woke Eden. However, even as the echoing notes died other noises came to the fore.

'Not again ... not fire ...'

She flew from the bed to stand in the darkness, not knowing where to find the light switch in the unfamiliar room. Cold air touched her bare legs. She tried to catch the smell of smoke. The strange whooshing sound took her back to the angry roar of flames as they reduced her kitchen to ash. *Don't shout – listen.* Eden held her nerve. Now she focused her attention on the sound to identify it. Fire? Unlikely: not so much as a whiff of smoke. Water gushing? No. It's not continuous. The whooshing's broken ... a rush-rush sound followed by silence.

Breathing?

No – snorting! That is someone – no, more likely an animal – breathing hard. Trying to catch a scent. What came to mind was a horse picking up a compelling aroma on the air. But why was it so loud in the house?

She pulled back the curtain to look outside. The rain

clouds had dispersed. A crescent moon, like a curving
steel blade, hung poised overhead. Its brittle light turned
a garden bush into a mass of silver speckles. As her eyes
adjusted she could make out the relentless black band of
the road slicing through fields. At the house it formed a
hook shape around the garden before flying toward
distant York. No traffic used it at this time of night. Then
that had always been the case when Eden visited as a
child. Sunset might as well have been a red stop sign for
this particular highway. A local man, who was
considered to be 'a bit slow', would immediately run
back to his parents' home in the village if he was caught
out alone on the road at dusk. Eden could still remember
vividly how he bellowed in fear as he ran, his arms
rotating in a fantastic windmill motion. 'Mam! Dad! I'm
frit … I'm frit!' Her grandmother explained that 'frit' was
a local word for 'frightened.'

Then she glimpsed a figure. It sped across the front
lawn. For a moment, she thought it was the man who
was scared of the road at night. She half-expected to hear
the terrified yell of 'I'm frit!' But the shape darted to the
base of the house. Then she heard the sound again.

'My God, he's smelling the door.' But the force of
that intake of breath? This was the peculiar thing: he
must be snorting great lung-fulls of air from the
building's interior. In astonishment, she murmured, 'He
wants to know what the inside of the house smells like.
Why on Earth would anyone do that?'

The figure, little more than a shadow, flitted lightly
toward the hedge, so it could look up at the bedroom
windows. Although Eden couldn't see properly, because
of the gloom, she formed the impression that its head
turned sharply from side to side as he searched the
house frontage. *For what? A way in?* She moved back

slightly so she was peering past the curtain, suddenly concerned that this strange entity might see her. The notion sent a shiver through her stomach. *He wants to get inside.* There was something distinctly odd about his movements. He didn't walk in a normal way. Shadow-man moved in a series of sudden, ultra-quick darts.

There, in the moonlight, a pair of silver lights. A split-second later Eden realised that they were a pair of eyes that stared in her direction. 'Oh, my God, he's seen me.' Eden recoiled back into the bedroom and her right heel slammed into the leg of the bed. Even as she grunted with pain she heard the noises again. This time they were preceded by a thump. Her imagination supplied the image of the stranger slamming his face against the edge of the front door, so eager was he to draw the scents of the house through the joints in the timbers, and suck them deep into his gaping nostrils. The snorting came even louder. The odours excited the trespasser. He found them as irresistible as a dog must find the musk of a bitch on heat. The rasp echoed up the staircase of the old house, then it raced into her bedroom as if to hunt her down.

Eden put her hands over her ears. *If I don't hear it, it can't get me ...* The thought darted from some part of her mind that still responded as a child. As she heard that snorting all those childhood fears of the dark came loping back. When the sound of nails being dragged down the door's woodwork joined the snorting, she screamed.

'Heather! Curtis! There's somebody trying to get into the house!'

She blundered toward the bedroom door. At that instant, she didn't want to put on the light. For it would become a guiding beacon for the intruder. No way in a million years would she signal which room for him to run to first. For what seemed like entire minutes, rather than seconds, she staggered along the landing in the dark, her hands feeling their way along. All the time, the sound of snorting – nothing less than a mauling of her nerves.

Then, when she was outside her aunt's bedroom, she slid her hands over the wall, trying to find the light switch. Eventually she chanced upon it and her fingers pressed the switch down. Light sprang all around her, blinding her. Squinting against its brilliance, she pounded on the door.

'Heather. Wake up! There's a man outside! He's trying to get in!'

'What!' Curtis swung open the door. His long gray hair stood out from his head in a spray of silver.

'What is it, Curtis?' Heather sounded only half-awake.

'It's Eden. She says –'

Eden interrupted, 'Hurry! He's trying to break the front door!'

This cut through the fog of sleep. Curtis's eyes were suddenly sharply awake. 'Wait here.' He padded swiftly along the corridor. When he spoke again it was in a whisper. 'Don't switch on the stairs' light. The front door's glass. I don't want him to see me.'

Despite him telling them to stay, Heather brushed past Eden to follow her husband. Eden didn't think twice. She stayed close to Heather as they padded down the stairs.

'What's that awful sound?' Heather asked.

'For some reason the man's smelling at door – like he's trying to get the scent of the house.'

'What on Earth for? That's a crazy thing to –'

From the foot of the stairs Curtis shushed them. He reached for the shepherd's crook that stood in a hallstand along with ornamental walking sticks. Once he'd armed himself he took two stealthy paces along the hallway toward the door.

Heather gasped. 'Oh my God, look at that!'

Eden followed Heather's pointing finger. The moment she saw what Heather indicated a deluge of ice cold shivers cascaded down her spine. Slowly, deliberately, yet with a sense of purpose, the trespasser at the other side of the door turned the handle.

Standing there in his pyjamas, Curtis tightened his grip on the staff. That was the instant that the moon brightened. It allowed them a glimpse of the menacing shape through the opaque glass panels in the door. Heather gave a low moan, almost of pain, as she saw how the man moved. His head revealed itself as a dark mass. It turned left and right as the man crouched to snort deeply along the edge of the door. During this he still continued to slowly turn the handle. Fascinated, they watched the black iron handle dip before returning to the horizontal. A smooth repetition, as if whoever tried to open the door couldn't understand that it was locked. The compulsive action of an idiot? Or relentless determination?

'Damn it,' hissed Curtis. He strode toward the door.

Heather lunged after him. *Don't go out there. Stay inside.*

Curtis grunted. 'He's disappeared anyway.'

Eden's mind raced. 'He won't give up yet. What if he's gone round the back?'

'I'll smash his skull with this.' Curtis tightened his grip on the staff. 'If he's got any sense he'll clear off now.' He opened the door to the lounge.

Eden saw the figure beyond the French windows flit through shadow. 'He's going round the back. He's looking for another way in!'

'Keep calm!' He all but screamed the words at her. 'Heather. Stay by the phone. If I give the word, call the police.'

'There isn't a police station for twenty miles.'

'Heather. Do it!'

A sense of impatience gripped her: husband and wife appeared on the point of standing there to bicker about what to do next. Eden skirted the couple before running down the hallway to the kitchen. There, the back door led out into the garden. She remembered this entrance consisted of a timber frame set with clear glass.

Without switching on the light, she ran lightly across the stone floor toward the door. Through the kitchen window she glimpsed a man-shaped shadow pass by. Despite the fear, a reckless need to see the man gripped her. That need burned itself into Eden's nerve endings. Suddenly *not* seeing him had become worse than gratifying herself with a clear view of the invader. Because already her imagination suggested the man wasn't what he seemed.

Before she reached the door, the handle began to turn. She flung herself forward in order to push her face to the clear glass, so she could see once and for all the kind of person who went round snorting at people's houses in the middle of the night.

Here, alas, the bulk of the house blocked the moonlight. Beyond the big pane of glass in the upper half of the door was only inky blackness.

'Who is it?' She pressed her face to the pane in order to see out. 'Who's there? I'm not afraid of you!'

Curtis burst into the kitchen. 'Eden! Come away!'

'You don't scare me!'

Then movement. Black moved against more black. Then white. All white. With a shocking abruptness.

Eden pushed herself back from the door. A crash rang in her ears. At the same moment she saw that the upper door pane had smashed. The glass turned frosty white.

Curtis shouted back to Heather, 'Call the police ... he's trying to smash his way in!'

Eden blinked: the violent attack on the door left her numb. She stared at the white pane that had been transformed into a sheet of crystals.

'Don't worry. You're safe,' Curtis told her. 'It's laminated glass. Like a car's windscreen. He can break it, but he can't get through. There's a plastic coating ...' He was panting as he drew her back toward the hallway. 'It's security stuff. The doors are reinforced, too.'

'So this has happened before?'

Curtis called back through the doorway. 'Heather. Have you got through to them?'

Heather appeared, her eyes staring with shock. 'What was that bang?''He tried to force his way through the glass in the back door. It's security grade laminate. He'll never get through that.'

'Where is he now?'

'I'm going to make sure I can see him. The little piece of vermin.' Curtis opened a cupboard on the wall to reveal a row of switches. He flicked them to unleash a cascade of light outside. 'We'll see if mystery boy likes to be floodlit!' Then Curtis dashed from window to window, this time the garden basked in illumination from halogen lamps. Soon he wore a broad grin. 'I thought that would sort him out.'

'Where is he?'

'Vamoosed. Gone. Skedaddled over the horizon. The coward.' Adrenalin had taken Curtis on a high. The grin became manic. 'God, I wish I could have got my hands on him. I'd have ripped the bugger's balls off.'

Heather seemed dazed. 'But why didn't the lights come on when he got close to the house? There's a sensor ...'

'Yes. The lights trigger when the sensor picks up body heat.'

'He must have tampered with the light.'

'No, no way. They're fine. Probably found a blind spot by pure chance.' He panted; his eyes were round as coins. 'You know something; I'm going to apply for a gun licence. Next time. Bang!'

Heather flinched at the word 'bang'.

Perhaps it was the way his wife flinched, because the adrenalin suddenly left Curtis. He stopped moving in that animated way. His flow of excited speech abruptly halted.

In that silence that was *more* than silence – almost like the vibration of a bell so vast that the note it made was too low for human hearing, yet powerful enough to be picked up by some sixth sense – Eden Page knew she had an important observation that must be spoken aloud.

Eden took a deep breath. These were words that had to be clear. 'Did either of you get a good look at the man? I didn't properly ... but wasn't there something wrong with his head?'

6

Tuesday Morning: 6.08

How Eden did it she didn't know. Immediately after the drama of the intruder attacking the back door she seemed so wide awake she'd never sleep. The last thing she remembered, however, was looking at the radio alarm clock beside her bed that told her the time neared one in the morning. It only seemed a moment later and she was opening her eyes to see that the clock read 6.08. A gleam of daylight edged the curtains. With the arrival of dawn the events of the previous night had the aura of nightmare, rather than reality. Once more she thought of the man who'd spoken to her on the train. *You should always respect omens ... beware, beware, beware ...* Even though she tried to not to dwell on what now seemed an ominous warning she knew it would be impossible to go back to sleep. What's more, recollections of the figure prowling around the house returned with vivid images of the man-shaped shadow. *And just what was wrong with his head?*

Eden went to the window to ease back the curtain. Admittedly, a little on the tentative side. What if the strange figure stood on the lawn staring up at her as she looked out?

There, in the grey light of morning, all that met her eyes was the immensity of the landscape. No strange intruder lurked on the lawn. Her eyes were drawn to where she had seen the figure. Nothing but sodden ground.

In this part of the world the flatness emphasised the hugeness of the sky. The fields were largely featureless. This blank land: it had the sullen expression of a thug, who stares at you with that same blank insolence as they stand in a bar, while you try and ease yourself by them. Yes, they share the same air of stupidity. It's like this drab realm could utter the same threat as the street thug. *I don't know you. You don't interest me. I can hurt you if I want. If I can be bothered. I might. Just to break the boredom. So beware, beware, beware ...*

'Talk about a lonely place,' she murmured. 'Why is it all so solitary looking? There's nothing in groups.' That misty greyness prompted her to mutter a litany. 'I can see one house, one tree, one road, a solitary church, a single scarecrow. A lonely pony. A lonesome rabbit. An individual post box. There are no families of bushes. No happy bands of rodents. Everything, but everything, is reduced to a miserly quantity of one.' Another fact occurred: 'Why is everything so straight? The fields all have straight fences, the dykes are straight, the paths are straight, the hedges are straight. The only thing bent is that road.' Her eyes followed that strange crook in the highway that meant it curled half way round the house almost like a python making a start on encircling its prey.

The *Via Britannicus* stretched way back into

history, as much as it stretched its hard body out across a gloomy land of rectangular fields that were either brown with dirt or dull green with vegetation. This view secreted an air of foreboding. Here bloody battles had been fought for possession of this flat-as-a-table-top realm. It suggested that the human suffering it had witnessed down through the ages had left it hardened, emotionally dead, it had felt blood spilt into its ground so often that, if it could have talked, it would say with a heartless shrug. 'Death again? So what?' Eden remembered what grim secrets these acres of mud had occasionally yielded. An ancient pot had been found at the road's edge that contained the cremated remnants of two people. Some bereaved Roman soldier had scratched on the pot in Latin, *'Meam uxorem. Meum infantem. Mithras! Oro illos protegere.'* – *'My wife; my young child. Mithras! I implore you to protect them.'* Captives were marched along the road in chains, bound either for slavery or crucifixion. Bandits hung from gibbets at crossroads as a warning to obey the law. Locals stole the bones of the hanged to magically blight the lives of rivals (at least, that was their intention). Far across austere fields, the ruins of the church became a little more distinct as the mist cleared. Savage winds that regularly tore across the plain from the cold North Sea had, years ago, robbed the building of its roof. No doubt local thieves had unburdened the House of God of its valuable lead flashing, too. A fierce infestation of ivy had defeated its walls. They had been reduced to half their original height as nature had sent vines between the carved blocks to push them apart. No families here. No friendly groupings. Not even of bricks. Mother Nature forced building blocks to become solitary stones. Another fifty years would see the earth suck what remained of the church into its uniformly moist, black dirt. Dog Lands conquered everything that came here.

As her eye followed the line of a path along a dyke she recalled her arrival yesterday. Seeing her aunt in the pit that resembled a grave. Eden fancied she could smell the soil again with its heavy odours of wet humus, peat, a lingering tang of burnt things. Strangely, it reminded her of a wine she'd once tasted that had been fermented in a stone vat in the basement of a Tuscan villa. The wine couldn't be described as pleasant; she'd grimaced as she tasted it. So heavy, so unnaturally sweet and a powerful intoxicant. It had made her head feel unnaturally large. When she'd stumbled outside to lie down in the shade of an olive tree all the colours of the world shouted at her, bird song shrieked through her skull, her tongue writhed in her mouth as even the scent of a rose struck her nostrils with such force that it left her clutching her face. In fact, clutching hard enough to bruise her skin. Recalling the wine, which smelt so much like the soil in the pit where the bones had been found, elevated her senses again. The landscape throbbed with the most intense browns and greens ... the dimensions of the scarecrow, the tree and the church ruin shifted. Time boundaries melted. For a moment she was ten years old again, stood by this very window, watching her mother running through the garden gate. Yes ... her mother had been doing something ... what was it now? Laughing? Screaming? Happy? Terrified? Eden could not remember or tell.

'Eden. You're never ever going to leave this place alive.'

The bedroom door toppled inward like a gravestone unseated from its earth. A vast, dark, unknowable shape rushed into the room. Pounced on her. Its huge mouth folded over her face. The heat of its gums seared like hot metal. As much as its teeth sinking into her cheeks was its overwhelming power to suck the air from her lungs and suffocate her. Choke her. Starve her of air.

Eden woke. For a while she lay there, letting her heartbeat return to normal. She couldn't tell where reality had ended and the nightmare began. The only fact she did know to be concrete was this: *I've passed the point of no return.*

7
Tuesday Morning: 8.00

'Can't Humpty's bones wait?' Curtis grimaced. He needed coffee fast, but the mug he had was far too hot. Today he'd dressed in a severe black suit. His silver pony-tail dangled, incongruously bohemian against the I MEAN BUSINESS garb.

'I need to find fragments of human skull. They simply aren't here.' Heather's fingertips danced through muddy splinters of bone on the table.

'I have to get into the studio early. I'm going to fire Wayne. He's staggeringly incompetent.'

Eden stepped through the door into Heather's lab.

'Good morning,' Curtis boomed. 'Sleep well?'

'Eventually.' For a moment she was uncertain whether to broach the subject of the intruder, the broken door pane, the figure with a head that seemed strangely *wrong. Don't tell me I dreamed it all.* Nevertheless, she found herself asking, 'What did the police say?'

'The police. Huh?' Heather examined a fragment of thigh. 'This belongs. It's human.'

'See, Eden? Humpty gets more attention than I do.'

Curtis swallowed coffee then swore under his breath. 'Oh, *that* ... After the idiot scampered last night I decided to call the police back and tell them not to bother coming out. There's no real harm done.'

'The door?'

'It's just one of those things. Some local kid got drunk, then got stupid. Happens. Glass is cheap enough. Remind me to call Bob. He can fix it today.'

Heather sighed with frustration. 'Skull. Skull ... Humpty, what on Earth did they do with your skull?'

Eden's skin prickled. She couldn't say how, or why, she knew but suddenly the truth glared at her with a power that sent shivers across her body. 'You won't find a human skull.'

'Tell me something I don't know. Ah, toe.' She plucked out a bone fragment.

Curtis downed another gulp of coffee. 'Didn't the garden centre want their accounts back by today?'

'All in hand, dear.' Heather studied a thick jaw bone bristling with sharp teeth. 'Canine. This goes back in the miscellaneous box.'

'No, it doesn't.' Eden took the brown mandible from her aunt. She placed it on the table at the top of the skeleton. 'It belongs there.'

'That's a dog's jaw bone, Eden. There's no doubt; it's –'

'The skeleton you found is complete!' The words rushed out of Eden with a quiet force that took Curtis and Heather by surprise. 'The skull bones you found go here.' She moved the shards that her aunt had dismissed as hound skull from the table's corner to where the head would be on the skeleton. 'Don't you see? The ground here is special. The road doesn't run straight through the plot where the house stands, because the Romans were obliged to go round something they venerated ... or feared.'

Curtis laughed. 'Heather. You've found another archaeologist in the making.'

'But one that needs some training in anatomy. Heather, the jaw isn't human.'

'It still belongs to this skeleton.' Her nerves tingled as she surged on. 'You found all those coins. They were offerings – sacrifices! – to the boy in the grave.'

'Deary me! The boy with the hound dog's head.' Curtis laughed louder.

Heather smiled, 'Really, Eden –'

'No, I'm serious. The Roman engineers understood. They diverted the path of one of their main highways. They knew better than to destroy the grave. What's more, they placed money into that pit above the grave. Later generations did the same. They made offerings of cash to the boy down through the centuries. What's more, they made sure that this grave, which was so special to them, wasn't disturbed.'

'Eden –'

'You showed me coins from Roman times, the medieval, Victorian, right through to the present day.'

Curtis drained his coffee; the amused expression was clear enough though. 'In effect, that old hole in our back garden was a slot for coins? So Humpty here could get rich in the afterlife?'

'You inherited your mother's imagination. I'll give you that.' Heather used her hand to carefully sweep the inhuman skull fragments to the side of the table. 'But you'll find there are no werewolves anywhere but in folklore and films.'

Curtis chuckled. 'I'd love to stay for the fun, but I've got some firing to do.'

'Listen, I'm serious,' Eden insisted. 'It's obvious, isn't it? What you have out there in the garden is an ancient shrine to someone special. A wizard or a god. The locals sacrificed money to whatever is in the grave for a reason. Hear me out, Curtis, they weren't frivolous or silly. They really believed that the person in the grave could give them something valuable in return for the money that they worked so hard for.'

'Your mother is a dreamer, too.' This time Heather's voice turned cold. 'It caused problems in the past. She could behave … stupidly. There's no easier way to put it, unfortunately. Yes, stupidly.'

'Boys don't have dog's heads.' Curtis stopped smiling. 'It just isn't possible.'

'I've been thinking about it,' Eden continued, exasperated by the couple's mocking responses. 'It's all makes sense. The whole area has dog-related names – this is Dog Star House in the village of Dog Lands. There's a Dog Dyke, Hound Flats –'

'Eden. You're getting carried away.'

'No, listen. I've been working it out. As well as references to dogs, you have to explain why an ancient road kinks to avoid something you can't even see on the surface. There are coins in the pit. These bones. Human, but instead of a human skull –'

Curtis grunted. 'Amusing as this is, I must go to the studio.'

'And then there was last night.' Eden's hair felt as if it stood on end as she said the words that had been lying heavy on her mind. 'Heather, you disturbed the grave. You brought the boy's remains into the house.'

Heather snapped, 'Eden, you're still upset after last night.'

'But what did happen last night?' Eden asked as

the pair glared at her across the table of burnt bones. 'Last night an intruder tried to get into the house. There was something wrong with his head.'

Curtis slammed his cup down. 'No, don't you dare. Don't you bloody dare!'

Eden protested, 'It makes sense. Just look at how all the facts add up.'

Curtis stormed from the room.

Heather followed her husband, but not before snarling, 'Thanks, Eden. Thanks a million. Now you've left me to pick up the pieces.'

8
Tuesday Morning: 10.00

Dog Star stood on its plot, at the bend of the *Via Britannicus*, beneath lumbering cloud. Heather worked on her dig. The awning that sheltered the tomb shifted in the breeze as if uneasy about being so close to the spot that yielded up those burnt bones. Eden watched her progress from the kitchen.

Eden hadn't spoken to Heather since her aunt had uttered *'Thanks, Eden. Thanks a million. Now you've left me to pick up the pieces'.* She watched her aunt haul a bucket of dirt from the pit. 'I should have listened to the man on the train,' Eden murmured to herself. She glanced at the door, its shattered safety glass held in place by the membrane of plastic. 'He told me, *You should always respect omens ... beware, beware, beware ...'*

She telephoned the builder. Could he start work on her apartment earlier? It would mean so much to her if he could. She was desperate to move back in.

'I'm sorry,' said the voice in her ear. 'I've still to finish this loft conversion job in Salford.'

'But you do know I'm homeless?'

'I can't just walk off a job. It wouldn't be fair.'

After the call she nearly talked herself into returning to the apartment anyway. Okay, the kitchen had been burnt. She could live off breakfast cereal, if need be. There was a café over the road. Only she recalled the smoke-blackened walls. And the stink. Even the thought of it made her throat feel as if had begun to swell in reaction to the stench of burnt plastic. *No. I can't go back there. Not yet.* Instead of destroying yet more bridges, she should start repairing some. She made coffee, then went out through the damaged door to face her aunt.

'For the last five years,' Heather told Eden abruptly, 'I have been struggling to persuade Curtis that this house should be our home. He wants to live in York. Last year a valuable sofa that he was storing for his father was ruined when the garage flooded. A week after that the airing cupboard door swung open at him. It left him with a gash in his head. He turns on me. He yells that the house is cursed. I've never seen him so furious. You wouldn't believe how hard it was to talk him out of leaving.'

Heather revealed this to Eden as they both stood beneath the gazebo. The pit yawned at their feet. Rain had left the soil darker than before. Oozing moisture, it smelt of burnt things.

Heather took a sip of the coffee that Eden had brought her. 'Now, this morning you brightly tell Curtis that we've got a damn werewolf sniffing at our front door.'

'I didn't use the word 'werewolf'. I just –'

'No, but you said this was the tomb of a boy with a dog's head.'

'Curtis won't believe in werewolves.'

68

'Maybe not, Eden, but that kind of speculation's hardly likely to endear him to the house, is it?'

Eden shook her head. 'I'm sorry. I thought you'd be interested in what I'd figured out.'

'Are you sure you've not got all this planned? A nice little scheme?'

'Scheme? What scheme?'

'Undoubtedly you know the terms of my mother's will. It stipulates that even though she left the house to me I can't sell it. Dog Star House stays within the family; it's chained to us. Tied lock, stock and bloody barrel. Dog Star? The will doesn't even allow us to change its stupid name.' She looked shrewdly at Eden. 'Tell me what happens to the house, then, if Curtis takes such a violent dislike to it that we have to leave?'

Eden shrugged.

'Surely, your mother – my sister – showed you a copy of the will?'

'I only heard that you'd inherited.'

'So you didn't know that I can't sell it? No?' Heather smiled, albeit coldly. 'Or that I'm legally obliged by the will to offer it for rent at a nominal sum to a specific chain of family members starting with my son? Graham won't take it because he's at sea all the time. Besides, living here bored him. Next in line is your mother. But she's such a free spirit she can't stay in any one place for longer than a couple of months straight. When she goes they'll have to concrete over her grave.' A joke, only Heather didn't smile. 'So who will be next in line to live in this house? And who would only be required to pay a few miserable pounds a month?'

'I'm not interested in the house, Heather.'

'It's a big property – five bedrooms; two bathrooms; new kitchen. If Curtis pushes me into leaving it's a certainty you'd end up living here in luxury. No doubt free to offer a bed to every psychopathic fire-starter that comes along.'

'Heather, that's not fair.'

'Okay. A deal. You stop telling Curtis that werewolves are laying siege to the house. I'll lay off your rotten choice of one-night stands.'

Heather glared at Eden in such a way that suggested she'd dash the coffee in her face if she disagreed. *What choice do I have?* Eden asked herself. *If I don't back off I'll end up on the train before the day's out. I've nowhere else to go.* Eden felt wronged by her Uncle and Aunt – the suggestion that she'd deliberately tried to scare Curtis into abandoning Dog Star House infuriated her – yet even after all this she knew she had no choice.

Eden took a deep breath. 'I wasn't trying to cause any trouble. Thanks again for asking me to stay here.' Even so, she couldn't back down completely: she couldn't surrender control over her own life entirely. She added with a splash of defiance, 'And I wasn't trying to steal your home from you.'

'Good. We have an understanding.' Heather's voice softened. 'Thanks for the coffee, by the way.' She nodded at the pit. 'It's like working in a fridge down there.'

Small talk. At least Heather was trying to mend bridges, too.

Eden leaned over the hole. The stench made her flinch. Wet earth. Decay. Burning. Something else that suggested a heavy sweetness. Talk about unwholesome. Even so, for some inexplicable reason the thick scent took her back to that Tuscan villa with its otherworldly atmosphere. 'Making any progress?'

'Just trying to get back to where I was when I

finished work last night. See the far side? Yesterday's rain caused part of it to collapse. I've got to lift out all the muck that's fallen into the bottom before I can start excavating again. And just when I'd reached the floor of a building, too.'

'Any more bones?'

'No.' Heather said the word a little too curtly, as if to dissuade Eden from reopening the dog-boy debate.

Oh, blood's thicker than water, Eden told herself. *Prove to Heather you're useful.* 'If you want, I could scoop out the dirt for you.'

This offer surprised Heather. 'Really?'

'Of course.'

'That would be a great help.' She sounded genuinely grateful. 'I've got to recheck the garden centre's accounts.'

'Just tell me what to do.'

'You will get your hands dirty.'

'No problem. I scrub up well.'

'Use the little ladder to climb down into the excavation. The sides are so soft you'll bring the lot down if you try to climb in or out any other way. There's a plastic bowl to shift the goo. I'd have suggested a spade normally but it might damage any finds. If you gently – gently, mind – scoop the debris out onto that plastic sheet. I can throw it into the flower beds once I've sieved it for hidden goodies. Sound good to you?'

Eden set to work. When she was standing in the grave pit, which once housed Humpty's bones, the ground was level with her shoulders. It took more effort than she'd appreciated to scoop wet mud into the bowl then stretch up and out of the hole to tip it onto the pile already started by Heather on the plastic sheet.

'How will I know when to stop?' Eden asked.

'When you're down to the hard surface. The floor of the building consists of stone slabs. I want you to go gently because they might have carvings, which could be fragile by now. Also, there's a slim chance there will be more tiles, too; maybe if we're really lucky a mosaic.'

After that, Heather returned to the house to her accountancy work. Eden worked hard to remove the invading mud. Yet her imagination still concocted fantasy portraits of dog-headed boys. She suspected they might once more creep into her dreams tonight. And, if they did, what marvellous secrets might they whisper into her ear as she slept?

9
Tuesday Morning: 11.30

A mound of soil that doesn't look particularly large can be surprisingly difficult to move. Especially when it has to be lifted above shoulder height before being dumped at arm's length. Eden's shoulders ached. Her arms had almost locked solid with exertion. The friction of the bowl against her fingers made the skin sore. Meanwhile, dirt from Humpty's grave smeared her hands. Her head rose above the lip of the pit before dipping below. At times she felt like a whale coming up for air before submerging again. The earth she shifted was more wet paste than individual grains. Each time her head lifted above ground level she sighed with relief at breathing fresher air. The wet odours of the pit bottom weren't appealing in the slightest. The outside world beyond the garden seemed uncannily distant now. As if the wall and the gate formed a barrier to a realm that she'd left behind. On the wall, very faded, but just legible, graffiti issued the brutal command: *Go To Hell!* Under normal circumstances, Eden would have noticed such unsettling vandalism straightaway, especially in this quiet rural garden; however, it was a measure of her anger at not being picked up by her aunt from the station that she missed it entirely when she first arrived. This place had that effect on one's emotions – it inflamed them. *What's more,* she mused, *did the graffiti suggest that Heather had fallen out with one of her neighbours?*

'I'm going to end up living out my life in this hole,' she murmured, half inebriated by the intense aroma of Humpty's grave soil. Maybe it was once a wine cellar in ancient times. *So much spilt wine soaked into the ground; amphorae of fermented grape; it's still here. Making me dizzy. Sending me daft as a loon …* She swayed, unsteady on her feet. *Now I'm lying in long grass … stalks become vines that threaten to strangle me. There is a river. And in that water are pear-shaped vessels … black liquid fills them … through the membrane I see shapes; they are squirming, all turning and squirming and pulsating … tiny arms … eyes that glare out at me …* The way the dream-like sequence oozed through her head induced a swirl of vertigo. *Where had those images come from? Is this place sending me crazy? It must be the lack of air in this Godforsaken pit. Oxygen deprivation. Exertion. That, and knowing that Dog Star House is going to burn, too. Just like my apartment burned …* Dear God. What had made her think such a terrible thing? Eden reached out both hands to dig her fingertips into the dirt sides of the pit. For an instant it seemed to her that she needed to grip the Earth itself. If she didn't, she might slip away from reality entirely, never to return. 'You're not used to exercise, my girl. You've let yourself go. Now, pull yourself together.' She'd spoken in a jokey way, imagining that it was her old gym mistress, scolding her again for lacking in gusto. Back then Miss Jericho briskly chided all her students for lacking 'gusto'.

Eden closed her eyes again and took a deep breath. She pictured Miss Jericho standing there in that white tracksuit she always wore, whistle in hand, and demanding that her girls scale the ropes again: 'But this time, when you climb, put some ruddy vinegar into it!'

When Eden continued digging, she put 'some ruddy vinegar into it', whatever that meant.

At the next dip of the bowl she glimpsed a hard object in the goo. 'No, don't you escape. You're my treasure.' She grabbed the piece of metal before it sank back into the mud. Gratefully, she lifted her head into fresher air. Here it was brighter, too, allowing her to examine her find. Little larger than her fingernail, another Roman coin. One side had become pretty much corroded beyond the point of no return but the reverse was remarkably clean. It revealed the profile of a bull-necked man with bulging eyes. 'Hail, Caesar.' She smiled, although it still felt goofy. The pong of the hole took her high as the stars.

'What in God's name are you doing?'

The sudden voice gave her a jolt. She spun in the grave pit to find the speaker. 'I didn't know you were there. You gave me a shock.'

A man of around sixty leaned forward over the gate, invading the garden's airspace, as it were. He stared at her with such a look of distaste that she tried to step backwards, her back coming up against the side of the pit. He clutched a checked cap in one hand. In his other, a carved walking stick. She noted that his thick woollen suit matched the gloomy meadows in that same dull green. One eye appeared weak, half closed; the other glared with such ferocity it easily made up for its partner's deficiency. If anything, his crowning glory was a formidable nose; this fantasia of bony architecture protruded from his face in a way that drew her gaze.

Angry, he pointed at the crater that Heather had

carved from the garden. 'I asked what you were doing?'

'Pardon?'

'What are you playing at? All this.' He jabbed a finger at the riven earth.

It's a dig ... an archaeological dig.'

'You can't ... you just can't.'

'This garden belongs to my aunt. She can do what she likes.'

'Oh no she can't ... not if you know the land. I was born here. Grew up in that farm yonder. My family have always worked the soil here.'

Was he suggesting that this was somehow his property? But Eden stuck to her guns. 'This house belonged to my grandmother. My aunt inherited it.'

'Ah ...' His one good eye examined her face. 'One of the Page family. I see it now. You all have the same jaw-lines. Hard. Very hard.'

She couldn't but help notice his prominent nose again. Was that a shared feature of the old farmer's family, too?

'I know Heather Laird, all right.' he said in a way that hinted of past battles with her. 'She's ... well, she knows what she wants.' His single good eye burned above the bridge of his nose. A surreal sun rising over a bony mountain. 'You're a smart looking girl. I can tell you've got common sense.' His voice adopted more friendly tones. 'But can you take a bit of neighbourly advice?'

'Depends what it is.' Eden sounded wary.

'Get out of that bloody hole. Go home!'

'I've got work to do. I'll have to say good-bye.' She climbed up the short ladder to exit the pit. *Return to the house,* she told herself. *Wait until the old grouch leaves.*

'Sorry. I didn't mean to be rude. But if I think

something I've got to get it said. I can see you're a nice lass. I only wanted to warn you ... it's for your own good. It wouldn't please me you getting into any kind of bother.' He shifted his stance so the walking stick took his weight.

After the experience of the midnight intruder this made her hesitate. 'What kind of bother exactly?'

'Well ...' he scraped the side of his nose with his fingernail. 'You should stop digging there for a start.'

'Why?'

'In the country it's not a good idea to dig too deep into the ground.'

'In case you disturb something that should remain undisturbed?' This was meant to be sarcastic. The man took it as a serious question.

'Aye. Farmers and the like, if they wind up with something that's bad they put it in the ground. They always have.' He issued his statement with utter conviction. 'Cattle with foot and mouth, anthrax, congestion of the lung. You bury the bodies. Same goes for contaminated feed, or when the government bans an insecticide or weed-killer. All of it goes in the ground. We pile rocks over it if need be. We keep it buried.' He tapped the walking stick as if to drive the ferule into the turf. 'It stays underground so it can't do any harm.'

'Thank you for the advice.'

'All I wanted was to give you a friendly warning. Digging holes is dangerous.'

Eden sensed he intended to slip away. *Not so quickly,* she thought, *you've given me reasons not to dig. That isn't the real warning, though, is it?* 'Last night someone came to the house.'

'Oh?'

'A stranger at midnight. He behaved oddly. He put

77

his face to the door as if trying to smell what was inside. After that he broke a window.'

'Did he get into the house?' The old man appeared genuinely concerned.

'Would you be worried if he had?'

His way of looking at her changed. He sensed now that she was aiming to extract facts that he wished to remain concealed. 'You're my neighbours,' he began. 'Here we look out for one another. There's thefts of machinery. Gangs come out from the towns.'

'Has it ever happened to you?'

'Six months ago a tractor got taken.'

'I'm not talking about thieves. I'm asking if you've ever had a stranger prowling around your property, smelling at the door like he's some kind of wild animal?'

The man wanted to leave now.

'Have you ever seen anyone like that?'

'No ... not at all.'

'You have, haven't you? What was wrong with the shape of his head?'

'Now then.' He breathed deeply. 'I've seen nothing like that. I don't know what you're driving at.'

'What did you think when you saw the head? How would you describe it?'

'I can't help you, Miss.'

'What was the first word that came into your mind to describe it?'

With some of his earlier conviction he came back with, 'Best keep your doors locked at night, then. Don't even look out the window. And take my advice: whatever you dug out of that hole put it back. Fill it up with soil. Turf it. Then leave well alone.'

'If the night visitor comes back, what should I do? Should I invite him in?'

'No!'

'Why? What is it?'

Heather's voice interrupted the beginnings of his reply: 'Now, what can I do for you, Mr Hezzle?'

The man's whole demeanour abruptly changed. 'Mrs Laird. Good morning. I've just been passing the day with your niece here. She's a good looking girl, isn't she?'

'Like me, she's not easily flattered.' Heather scowled. 'Have you been letting your dogs run wild again, Mr Hezzle?'

'They can go where they please on my land.'

'They're brutes, Mr Hezzle.' The woman kept her voice formal; even so, there was more than a hint of irritation. This must be the source of a long running argument. 'You should keep them tied up in the farmyard, if they're not allowed in the house.'

'Everyone here has dogs,' he replied evenly. 'If you call out the police today they'll appear next Tuesday – if you're lucky. Those dogs of mine keep thieves away. We'd be robbed bankrupt if it weren't for those brutes, as you call them.'

In a telling way she sang out, 'Good day, Mr Hezzle.'

With polite restraint he nodded a farewell, then in a more friendly way to Eden, 'Take care of yourself, Miss.' A moment later he walked vigorously away.

'He's one of the notorious Hezzle tribe,' murmured Heather to Eden. 'They say they've been here since … well, from before the Romans marched in, if you believe all the tales they tell you. Take my advice, have nothing to do with them.'

'Mr Hezzle was giving me some advice.'

'What? The one about leaving bread and milk at

your back gate at sunset? Or never cut the holly bushes down in your garden?' 'Mr Hezzle told me not to dig holes.'

'That's a novel one, I suppose.' She checked the excavation. 'Good work. You saved the day, Eden. Will you help me lift one of those stones at the bottom? There might be an earlier floor beneath it.'

After that there was only small talk. Eden looked round the garden.

'You don't have any holly bushes?'

'No, I can't stand them. We had all the holly ripped out.'

10
Tuesday Afternoon: 5.45

Curtis arrived; an angry whirlwind in human form. He slammed the car door, kicked open the front door to Dog Star House. Then ripped open kitchen cupboards.

'Why can I never find anything in this house!'

Heather tried to keep pace with him. 'Curtis? What have you done to your face?'

'I've done nothing to my face. He's going to pay for this!' He smashed a cupboard door shut. 'What is it with this house? The moment you want something – *need something!* – it hides away!'

'Curtis. Let me have a closer look.'

Eden stood in the doorway.

'Yes, Eden. You join the audience. Have a really good look at this!' He pointed to his face. 'I told Wayne he was sacked. The ungrateful little sod took a swing at me.'

'It might need a stitch.' Heather held his head between her two hands as she examined the cut that ran through an eyebrow. Blood smeared the skin up into his hair line. There, dried blood formed brown crumbs amongst the silver strands.

'A stitch. Does it hell need a stitch. I just need the first aid kit.' He jerked his head free of his wife's hands.

'Eden,' Heather said, 'There's antiseptic cream and plasters in the bathroom cabinet.'

'I'll be right back.' Eden hurried up the stairs.

In the kitchen Curtis raged, 'I'll call Raj tonight. He can issue the summons. I'll have Wayne in court so fast the little idiot won't know what's hit him!'

11
Friday Morning: 8.20

Several things happened that Friday morning. At least 'things' that, to Eden, hinted at momentous events to come.

Firstly, Curtis left early for the studio. With grim satisfaction written large on his still-bruised face, he snarled, 'I wish I could see Wayne's ugly mug when the court papers are served on him. If he thinks he can take a swing at me, he can think again.'

Secondly, dark clouds swelled in the sky. Thunder grumbled on the horizon. An ominous threat of approaching storm.

Thirdly, Heather announced that continuing the dig today would be pointless because of the rotten weather forecast (frankly, the gazebo offered scant shelter when it came to torrential downpours). 'Instead, you can help me shift some of the junk out of the attic. I should have done it after my mother died, but I didn't fancy tackling it on my own. Now I've got you it's time I rolled up my sleeves.'

Fourthly, Eden Page had a revelation. *So now they're*

treating me as a servant. I'm no longer the guest. I'm the live-in help. They expect me to obey their commands. In desperation she telephoned the builder again. No, he couldn't start work on her apartment until the end of the month. No escape yet. Unless …

Eden telephoned her mother. Or at least she tried. Only after calling half a dozen of her mother's acquaintances did Eden learn where Mum had gone. She had headed out to Dublin to stay with a friend. Mum being Mum there was no contact number of course; no address, no e-mail access. Eden's mother feared that mobile phones, like permanent addresses, pension schemes and marriage, were all instruments of confinement. *A free spirit, my old Mum. Bless her.* Being unable to contact her mother brought Eden to item *Five:* 'I'm alone,' she murmured as she washed the breakfast dishes. 'I really am alone.'

'What was that, Eden?' called her aunt from the living room where she sat and leafed through a magazine.

'Nothing. I'm only singing to myself.' *Why did I say that? I should have told Heather that I'm sick of being treated like a serving maid. No, it's more than that: I feel so alone here. I've not a single friend within thirty miles. And neither you nor your grouch of a husband really want me here.* Homeless or not, she could see herself launching a verbal attack on both her aunt and uncle before the day was out. She'd tell them what a low opinion she had of the pair. Then whatever happened she'd catch the train back to the civilisation. 'This place is driving me mad,' she hissed as she pulled the sink plug. For a moment she imagined herself as a bird hovering high above Dog Star House. Roman road at one side. Flat, endless fields all around. Besieging the place. Jailed by circumstance rather than high walls. *This isolation. It's crushing …*

12
Friday Morning: 11.00

Any effective work at clearing the attic of unwanted junk came to an end with the discovery of the documents.

'My mother's ,' Heather announced. 'I remember when I was a young girl my mother always saying that she wouldn't allow her brain to go to seed living out here in the middle of nowhere.' Heather pulled files from a box. 'She got a bee in her bonnet about this. Night after night she'd sit at the kitchen table bashing away at a portable typewriter.'

'What language is it?' Eden peered at a clutch of handwritten pages.

'Latin. The typescript is the translation. What made her so obsessed with it I'll never know, perhaps sheer loneliness. After all, for years your grandmother and I were the only people living in the house.'

They sat side by side in the attic on an old steamer trunk that bore stickers announcing its travels to places like Alexandria, Cape Town and Hong Kong. In the attic were boxes of Christmas decorations, an exercise bike (no longer used), vac-pacs of clothes and stacks of rural life magazines. Eden angled a typewritten file so the light from the bulb fell on it.

'It must have taken years,' Eden marvelled. 'There's hundreds of pages.'

'The fruits of an obsessive,' Heather sighed. 'Sometimes people can become fixated on the oddest passions.'

Like you excavating your own garden. Five minutes ago, Eden Page would have pointed out Heather's obsession, too. This file, however, interested Eden. It suddenly seemed important, even if she couldn't explain why.

'So what is this?' she asked. 'A novel?'

'No. Daisy, your whimsical, pixie of a mother, has all the imagination in the family. I was only about eight when my mother stopped work on this. All of a sudden if I remember rightly. As if it made her angry. Perhaps she realised it had been frivolous.' She picked out more files from the box. 'Every day my mother went to the church where the village archive is kept. The documents go back centuries; lots of them are in Latin. My mother took it on herself to translate them. These are records of marriages, births and deaths. Look, this page is for December 1642.' She began to read a section highlighted in red. '"Moses Grander, his wife Susan, seven daughters and two sons died, twenty third day of December as a result of inundation; Dog Dyke End water mill."' Heather rifled through the box. 'See, there's more of it. File after file. Sheesh. This is a register of parish priests going back to 870 AD.'

'Can you find the most recent file?'

'Does it matter?'

'If your mother stopped work all of a sudden perhaps she learnt something that troubled her.

Whatever it was, it'll be in that last file.'

'Eden, don't we have an agreement? You stop the Werewolf talk. I'll lay off how your apartment caught fire.'

'Did I mention the word "Werewolf"?'

'Just a warning.'

'If anything, I thought she might have discovered some secret that was an embarrassment to the village.'

'Eden, I strongly suspect the reason she stopped work on this was because she became pregnant with your mother. Even before she was born Daisy was trouble. My mother was so sick most mornings she couldn't get out of bed, never mind translate volumes of Latin into English.'

'Were you bitter about my mother being born?'

In lieu of answer Heather delved into the box again. 'According to the date this is the latest. See, she'd written the month and year on the file.' Heather read the title. '"*The First English Translation of* The Secular and the Sacred Balk of Elmet; *subtitled:* The Hermit of Kirkhampton's History of our Village". Ah ... this must be the last file my mother worked on. See, it's just a mass of rough jottings. If anything, it's mainly chapter headings from the Hermit's book, which, according to this was written by a local man in 1488.' Heather leafed through the notes reading at random. '"Chapter 21: The importance of avoiding women. The scourge of carnal affection. Chapter 25: An explanation on the reasons why desire of the world and of womankind is to be detested. Tears which are turned into music." Ah ha. "Women for kitchen hearth and birthing" ...' Heather smiled. 'It's fairly obvious what the dear old Hermit thought about our sex.'

Eden spoke with utter conviction. 'But your

mother – my grandmother – learned something from the Hermit's book, which had a profound effect on her. She stopped all work on the translation.''You might be right, Eden. But if it's here I don't see it.' Heather turned the pages. 'Although take a look at that. My mother was doodling in church.'

Here was a sketch on one page devoted to translating a hymn that ran *Make my flesh free of earthly love.* The drawing of people, sitting in pews before a priest pointing skyward, had been titled *Our Happy Congregation, Harvest Festival, 2nd October 1968.*

'We always used to go to church on Sundays,' Heather sighed. 'I never saw Mum sketch this, though. "Happy Congregation" is meant to be a joke of course, just look at these lines above the people. She drew steam coming out of their heads to show how angry they are.' She studied the doodle more closely. 'Good heavens, she's drawn the villagers like gargoyles.'

'No, these aren't caricatures. Look at the size of their noses. She's drawn Mr Hezzle's family.'

'Goodness, I think you're right. I'd bet good money that the chap at the end shaking his fist is Albert Hezzle, the man you met a couple of days ago. A lot younger here, of course. This sketch was done over forty years ago. And he's still as grumpy. My Mother wasn't a bad artist. She's caught the mood all right. They're not happy about what the Vicar's telling them.'

'Go right to the end of the file. See what the last notes are before she stopped.' Eden surged on with an additional, 'Or before she *was* stopped.'

Heather gave Eden a curious sideways glance but said nothing. 'It's still chapter headings and fragments of the Hermit's verse.'

'Which prove he was a life-hating, world-hating

misogynist.'

'Absolutely …' Heather worked her way to the last page. 'Ah, here's something.' Her voice rose in surprise. 'Dog Star House! It's about this place. My God.'

'But the house wouldn't have been built in the middle ages.'

'No. It's about what stood here before.'

'Then this must be important. Your mother was preparing to do a lot of detailed work on the translation. Only for some reason she didn't get any further.'

'Like I said. Morning sickness. In spades.'

'No, I don't believe that. Your mother was onto something. Mr Hezzle warned me about digging holes in the garden.'

'Mr Hezzle's a –'

'No, this is important.' With Heather's no doubt derogatory assessment of the old farmer brushed aside, she added, 'Look at all these words here. Your mother was searching for the right translation of a particular phrase. This must have been key to what was happening here. She took pains to get it right. See: *Homo Prima*. Then there's different attempts at turning the phrase into English.' She quickly read the list as a tingle of excitement ran through her. '"*Homo Prima*. First Man. Original Man. Premier Man." Look: "First Man" is underlined twice.'

'"First Man"? That's probably a title for the male head of a family or a tribe.'

Eden tilted her head to see something scrawled in a margin. 'The First Man is connected with the site of this house. Here's some notes: "H demands Bishop conduct exorcism on Dog Star Hook. Bishop accedes."' Eden mouthed the cryptic sentence again to herself, 'H? H for Hermit I suppose. Dog Star Hook?'

'That's what locals call the bend in the road. The one that makes it curl half-way round the garden before it runs straight again.'

'So the Hermit believed this land was haunted. He wanted the Bishop to banish the ghost.'

Heather bit her lip. Clearly she wanted to know more, but Eden suspected that she'd resist any more talk of werewolves and the supernatural. Instead of speculating about a rite of exorcism being conducted on this plot of land, she continued reading the note that must have been jotted in a hurry. '"Rolands arrive" … Rolands?'

'"Romans arrive",' Heather corrected. 'Her handwriting's a bit wild.'

Eden read on, '"Romans arrive Yorkshire first century, commanded by" … I can't read that. Grandma must have been shaking with excitement as she wrote this.'

'Ahm … General Gallus.'

'"… General Gallus, plus legion's soothsayer, identifies *Homo Prima*" – the First Man – "as living embodiment of entire pantheon. Orders re-routing of *Via Britannicus* to spare theo … theo …" what's that word?'

'Perhaps "Theopolis"? Not a real word, but suggests "city of god". Or at least a place where the god or gods live.'

'"General Gallus makes extraordinary visit to Emperor Claudius. Secures Imperial directive that First Man be venerated by Roman Army. Feast day set June 3rd. Coin struck in First Man's honour. Emperor announces day of games in Rome in celebration. Free bread for poor. Gallus promoted."'

'Phew …' Eden's aunt could often appear too cynical for her own good; this time she was genuinely impressed. 'You know what this means, Eden? The general invaded this part of Yorkshire nearly two thousand years ago. For some reason he had an epiphany when he reached this very spot. Right where this house is built! He believed he'd found the city of the gods. The legion's holy man agreed. So, not only does General Gallus order that the road be diverted to preserve whatever he found, he makes a special trip back to Rome because he was so excited. He had to tell Emperor Claudius in person.'

'Claudius believed him?'

'Absolutely. Because he promoted Gallus, had a commemorative coin struck, and then held a colossal party in the city to celebrate the discovery. The poor even got free grub. This was the king of shindigs – a national festival of thanks.'

'But what made this place so important?'

'Important? It is amazingly important.' Heather's eyes shone with excitement. 'The most powerful man in the Roman Empire, Claudius, knew he'd been given the location of Theopolis. The city of the gods here on Earth.'

'No ... that isn't what it says. Not exactly.' As Eden started to speak the phone rang downstairs. 'It says here that –'

'Eden, I best get that. It might be the garden centre about their accounts.' Heather rose to her feet from where she'd been sitting on the steamer trunk.

Eden knew this was important; she needed to press this one fact, at least, well and truly home. 'But the full sentence reads: "General orders re-routing of *Via Britannicus* to spare Theopolis that exists inside the body of the First Man."' She sighed with frustration as Heather hurried toward the attic ladder.

'Heather. This is important.'

'Later. I've got to take the call.'

Heather descended the ladder as Eden called out. 'Don't you see? It's not saying there was an actual town here. It's stating categorically that the city of the gods *exists inside the body of the First Man.* How can a holy city be inside a person?'

'I'll be back in five minutes. We'll talk then.' The phone's ring was insistent. 'I'm coming, I'm coming ...' Heather ran down the stairs.

Eden returned to the file. What she learned there on the last page prompted her to carry the file downstairs. Not to find her aunt. Instead, she hurried to the lab to look once more at Humpty's bones.

13
Friday: Noon

Eden Page worked on arranging the bones. Heather had already laid out the rest of the skeleton on the table – collarbone, ribs, pelvis, thigh bones, shin, the tiny pebble shaped bones of the ankle. Most were charred, which left a black scale. The stink of burning still pricked her nostrils. What occupied Eden now were the shards of skull. She retrieved the canine remains from the bowl marked 'Miscellaneous', then carefully, painstakingly, with a furrowed brow, she assembled the skull fragments – the dog-like jaw complete with incisors, the thick brow ridge, the smoother, broader plates of the crown of the head.

As she worked, she murmured a nursery rhyme to herself : *'Humpty Dumpty sat on a wall, Humpty Dumpty had a great fall. All the king's horses, And all the king's men, Couldn't put Humpty's* bones *together again.'*

Heather entered with the bright announcement, 'Coffee.' Then she saw Eden's handiwork. 'Damn you, Eden! I told you not to do that. Are you really intent on pulling some kind of stunt to scare Curtis away? This is our home. I won't let you drive us out, you bloody monster!' She slammed the cups down on the desk hard enough to splash half the contents out. Then she advanced on her niece as if ready to punch her. 'Get away from that!'

'No, hear me out.'

'I'm warning you. Bloody werewolves? You think I'm stupid?'

'You've had trouble before, haven't you?'

'I'm not discussing that with you. Put those skull fragments back in the bowl.' Heather bunched her fist.

Eden stood her ground. 'I won't. And you are going to listen to me. I've been working it out. I'm starting to understand.'

'Eden! Get the damn train back to wherever you came from.'

'Heather.' Eden spoke with utter conviction. 'You didn't read your mother's notes properly. General Gallus described the First Man as the Theopolis. That the city of gods was *inside* of him. The General also stated that he was the living embodiment of the pantheon. Do you see what he was driving at?'

'Take the skull bones away, then we'll talk.' Despite her anger Heather was intrigued. 'You might have thought doing that was a joke. Let me tell you, it's –
'

'Heather, listen. You've had trouble here before, haven't you?'

'*Yes* ...' It pained Heather to admit it. Even then she quickly dismissed its importance. 'Just Hezzle's farm dogs. They were running amok. Making a hell of a mess in the garden. Scratching. Gnawing the car, for heaven sakes.'

'You saw Mr Hezzle's dogs?'

'We didn't have to. It was obvious they were his. Savage things they are.'

'So you never actually saw them attacking the garden?'

'Does it matter? Please, Eden. Before Curtis gets home put the skull fragments back in the bowl, and whatever happens don't mention the word "werewolf".'

'I won't even breathe the word "werewolf".' Eden spoke with confidence. 'Besides, this skull has nothing to do with dogs or werewolves.'

'Amen to that.' Heather's relief was heartfelt. 'Another mention of werewolves and I'd scream, God help me, I would.'

'Look, just bear with me for moment.' Eden picked up her grandmother's file. 'First, the sketch of the congregation. Back in 1968 they are genuinely angry. They have just been told that my grandma – your mother – is translating that odious religious zealot's book. Mr Hezzle and the rest knew about the Hermit's life-hating, woman-hating mission. They also know full well that this bigot petitioned the local Bishop to conduct rites of exorcism on the land in 1488. Some bones were dug up by the Bishop's priests, burnt, then reburied. He also had the Bishop come to the parish church here in Dog Lands to tell the congregation that the First Man was evil, ungodly, the worst kind of pagan. In fact, he went through the First Man's teachings point by point in order to rubbish them. But then the Bishop finished his speech to the locals with what he believed would be the clincher. The killer blow that would make everyone despise the First Man.'

'And that was?'

'See for yourself. It's here before you.' Eden nodded at the table.

Heather's eyes widened. 'You're saying the skeleton really is complete?'

By way of reply Eden read from the file. '"The Bishop struck the lectern as he cried out in a fierce voice: *How can any right thinking person of this Kingdom believe the words of a man that wears the head of an ape?"*'

'This is the skeleton of the First Man?'

'And it's his skull. Only it's not a dog's skull. It's superficially dog-like maybe. But then apparently baboons have heads that resemble a dog's.'

'Poor devil. Then he was deformed?

Eden leaned forward to gaze into the eye sockets of the broken skull. 'A deformed man, who a Roman general identified as having the city of the gods inside of him? Something that excited the Emperor so much that nineteen hundred years ago he declared this "poor devil", as you put it, be worshipped?'

'That must be it.'

'No, it's not the whole story.'

'You found this out from my mother's notes? They were just random jottings. Nothing coherent.'

'I found this at the back of the file.' Eden unfolded a sheet of paper covered with fierce handwriting. There was so much ink it seemed to obliterate every square inch of white. 'It's a letter from Albert Hezzle, dated 4th October, 1968: two days after the same harvest festival where your mother sketched the congregation's anger, when the vicar told them about the translation of the zealot's book. The villagers hated the Hermit. They loved the First Man.'

Heather stared at the letter as if it smouldered in Eden's fingers, just about to burst into flame and consume them all. 'My mother received that letter, then stopped work on the translation?'

Eden nodded.

Heather turned back to the skeleton. 'It seems as if Humpty, or more correctly the First Man, still wields influence.'

'Do you know why?'

'They're a superstitious lot round here. A perceived bad omen can put the wind up them.'

'No, as I told you, it's not fear that the First Man inspires … it is Love.'

Her aunt shrugged. 'So? He's dead. Long, long dead.'

'But something lives on.'

'What? His wandering spirit?'

Eden shook her head. 'His teachings.'

'They'll be of academic interest to historians. That's all.'

'According to Mr Hezzle's letter the First Man's knowledge is very much alive – albeit locally – and is something of a village secret. What's more, the Hezzle family hoped that one day all of humanity will receive what they term "the Gift".'

'"And as soon as we receive this marvellous Gift, humanity will be saved",' concluded Heather with sigh. 'If we had a golden nugget for every religion that's promised salvation of our eternal souls …'

'It's not about souls and the after-life. The First Man's Gift would apparently improve the quality of life here on Earth.'

'That's very laudable. But undoubtedly delusional.'

'According to grandma's notes and Mr Hezzle's letter, which is incredibly detailed, I've worked out the jist of …' Eden nodded at the bones on the table, '… the nature of his Gift.'

'And?'

'The First Man would father the children of local women. By the hundred, or even the thousand.'

They both looked up as thunder rumbled in the distance. A sound suggestive of prowling menace.

'Ah, sex.' Heather gave a knowing smile. 'I should have known that the Gift of any self-proclaimed male hero would involve a stonking, great harem, so he could enjoy unfettered shagging rights.'

Thunder growled again. It grew darker inside the room as storm clouds loomed above the dreary expanse of fields. A car took the bend in the highway just a little too quickly. Its tyres squealed in protest. A moment later it accelerated safely away from the evil crook in the road.

Eden shook her head. 'You might be a cynic, Heather, but local people, just like the Romans, believed in the First Man's Gift.'

She turned back to the skeletal puzzle on the table and completed the brow ridge above one eye with a fingernail-sized fragment of bone that fitted perfectly. The face didn't seem to resemble a dog so much now. Instead, something else emerged.

Eden spoke fluently, confidently: 'The followers of the First Man realised this important fact: that the children he fathered with local women grew up to be superior to other children. They were stronger, more intelligent, more resistant to illness, and enjoyed a much longer life-span.'

'So why did the Roman general describe the First Man as the Theopolis?'

'Because General Gallus talked to him. Gallus possessed an enquiring mind. He knew that each Roman god and goddess had their own special talents: Mars, the god of war; Juno presided over marriage and children;

Saturn, the god of agriculture. As you know, the Romans believed there was a whole bunch of deities in heaven. Gallus figured out that these godlike talents, or more accurately "fields of expertise", had become fused into individuals known as the First Men. Hence, the title. The First Man would become the first in a long line of super-intelligent individuals with increased longevity. In turn, these would then sire more children.'

Heather gave a long, low whistle. 'So a race of supermen would be born. And, in turn, the eventual extinction of *Homo Sapiens.*'

In the growing gloom, shards of ancient Roman pottery stood out as splinters of orange, as they caught the failing light. Eden noticed fragments of faces gazing from yet more remnants of bowls and jars that once contained spices, wine, and scented oils from Persia, and, perhaps, funerary unguents borne from mysterious realms along the Great Silk Road that linked the Orient with Imperial Rome. Once more thunder growled; this time with enough force to make a window pane shiver.

Heather shuddered. 'We're in for storm. Out here they can be a real nightmare. I hope Curtis comes home soon.' Then she looked directly at Eden. 'You know. I thought at first you were like your mother. I admit I was wrong. You are intelligent. You've examined all the facts you could find, then you worked out the truth. You'd have made a first class detective. I mean that sincerely, Eden. I'm impressed.'

'I can also deduce that you don't like my mother. That you think she's silly.'

'I didn't say that.'

'No, but I can piece your opinion together ... just like these bones. Look at this,' she moved to the table and gently touched the cheek of the skull. 'The First Man

didn't have the head of a dog, or an ape. He was a man
… but a man from a difference species.'

14
Friday Evening: 7.30

Thunder. Still no rain.

Curtis detested his day. He prowled; he snarled. Four times he made telephone calls. Complaints, expressions of frustration. With Curtis's angry mutterings came more thunder. Plenty of thunder, a hollow sounding boom in the distance; the sound of massive barrier walls collapsing. When he poured himself a huge glass of merlot, the colour of blood in this half light filtering through grim slabs of cloud, he made his fifth call.

'Raj? Raj! You were going to get those damn court papers organised. No, that's not good enough. I want Wayne's ugly face in court. I want to see him go through hell after what he did to me.' He touched his bruised eye. 'Get it done Monday. Okay? That's all well and good … yes … if the papers aren't served next week you'll be losing a valuable client. Goodbye.' He glowered through the window. 'Bloody weather.' He emptied the wine down his throat then went for a refill.

Curtis jabbed a glance at Eden as she brought him

a plate of sandwiches. He chose to interpret her expression the wrong way. 'I can drink whenever I want. It's my blasted house.' He glared at his wife. 'Even if my name isn't on the deed, it's still my home.'

'Have you chosen a replacement for Wayne?'

'I've been too busy dashing round sorting out all his cock-ups. Did you know he hasn't bothered to confirm bookings for Thursday and Friday next week? The studio will be lying idle for two full days. At this rate we might as well rent it out to a farmer to store his spuds. We'd earn more.' He drained his glass and refilled it again, reaching the end of the bottle. 'Is it me,' he muttered with no trace of humour, 'or are wine bottles getting smaller? This didn't last two minutes.' He headed for the kitchen like he dearly wished he could find some underling there to thrash within an inch of their life.

More thunder broke across the horizon. Still no visible lightning; no rain either. The daylight took on a greenish tinge as it seeped through thick cloud.

Eden and Heather sat and looked at each other in silence. Each lost in their own thoughts.

Heather had taken several bites of her sandwich, and was chewing listlessly when she swallowed, frowned and stiffened. 'He's been a long time.' She called out in the direction of the living room door. 'Curtis? Everything all right through there?' She stood up, 'Curtis?'

Eden listened. 'I think he's gone through to your lab.'

On the word 'lab' Curtis punched open the door. His face seemed to pulsate with rage. 'What the hell are you playing at with this?' He brandished the fragments of skull that Eden had glued together. 'Is it meant to be a joke? Is it?'

'Curtis,' Heather began. 'I planned to tell you later.

We've made a real breakthrough about this site. Did you know that nearly two thousand years –'

'I'm not interested. I've got real problems! I've got trouble with cash flow, with staff, with yawning great bloody gaps in studio bookings. All you do is make freaks out of old bones.' He turned on Eden. 'Idiot girl! I warned you about this ridiculous idea about werewolves and dog men. This is our home! Not a venue for your moronic, make-believe games.'

'Curtis!' Eden fired back with equal vigour. 'It's not make-believe. It's not werewolves. Heather and I have found out about this place. It was sacred ground to the Romans.'

'I don't believe I'm hearing this. My business rates are overdue. I get assaulted by my own staff. And you babble about sacred ground. Listen, this is our home, an ordinary house built on ordinary dirt. And I've got to earn money to pay for its upkeep.'

'But it is important. We found out that Heather's mother was warned off from researching its history. The locals want to keep what happened here a secret.'

He brandished the section of rebuilt skull, with the thick eye ridge above vast eye sockets. 'I'm warning you both. No more of this. Okay? Eden, there's a train at eight in the morning. You're going to be on it.' He ripped the glued pieces of bone in two with his bare hands, his eyes blazed. At the same time, thunder smacked against the house like a bomb. 'Now I'm throwing this in the bin. The rest of the blasted bones are joining it.'

He pounded out of the house. Heather ran after him, pleading that he calm down. Eden followed. A sense that events were running out of control gripped her now. *The brakes have gone*, she told herself. *We're falling over the edge. Curtis can't control himself. He's going to hurt someone*

... he's going to hurt us!

Outside, the crash of thunder became even more violent. A cacophony that made Heather clutch the side of her head. They pursued Curtis across the garden to where he flung back the lid of the wheelie-bin.

'You might as well watch this!' Fury as well as drink flushed his face crimson. 'I'm not taking any more!'

Before he could hurl the bones into the bin full of discarded cartons, pizza crusts, and potato peelings he stopped. His eyes looked past the women, locking onto something behind them.

Eden spun round to see what it was, only whatever it was moved far too swiftly. An impression of a flitting shadow; nothing more.

Curtis stared, his eyes bulging. Even he wasn't sure what he'd seen. Only it had been enough to stop him dead. He'd gone from rage to silence in one second flat.

Heather had been the last to notice. 'What is it? What's wrong?'

'Something came across the lawn,' Eden breathed.

'What?'

Curtis recovered from his surprise. 'Eden, did you see that?'

'Not clearly.'

His anger flared. 'Some idiot ran through those bushes. What on Earth are they playing at?' He'd forgotten all about the pieces of skull in his hand now. Instead, he advanced toward the shrubbery. Almost to himself he said, 'But did you see how fast he ran? Like a hare!'

Heather caught her husband by the arm to prevent him plunging headlong into the vegetation. 'Curtis, hold on. Did you see who it was?'

He shook his head. 'I only half saw. Nothing properly. A shape ... just a hell of a fast one.'

'I'm glad I found you.' A figure bustled through the garden gate.

Curtis groaned. 'Hezzle. I should have known. If it's one of your blasted mutts ...'

Mr Hezzle's eyes were huge in his head. Even the weak one that had barely opened when Eden first met him seemed to poke right out from the socket, a veined orb with a fierce black pupil. 'Back to the house ... inside ... quick!'

'What?' Curtis had no intention of moving.

'Get into the house. Straight away ... go on, get inside. Lock all the doors.' Despite his advanced years, he ran past Heather's excavation pit. 'Inside, quick! Lock the doors!'

There was something about his manner. An utter conviction that somehow sent them back through the door into the kitchen. Mr Hezzle didn't so much as follow as push them indoors. Once they were safely in he slammed the door shut behind them.

'Lock it!' He shouted so loud that the thunder seemed tame in comparison. Eden moved fastest, she shot the bolts across top and bottom.

Mr Hezzle sucked air through his large nose, his chest heaved. 'Are all the other doors locked? Windows, too?'

'What is this?' Curtis spat the words. 'This is *my* hou –'

'Lock them.'

'I'll do it.' Eden flew round the ground floor. Fortunately all were locked. A moment later she was back in the kitchen to find Mr Hezzle drawing the blinds.

'Hezzle. Tell us what on Earth is going on!' Curtis was on the verge of committing violence.

'He's out!' Mr Hezzle slammed his hand down on the kitchen table. 'He knows you took the bones from the mausoleum!'

Curtis snarled. 'Mausoleum? What the hell are you talking about?'

The old man turned to Eden, 'The lass knows. She told me he came here this week. He sniffed at the doors. He could tell the bones were inside. She said he tried to break in.'

The eyes of her uncle and aunt flicked to the smashed security glass in the door.

'It was just some local drunk,' Curtis snapped. 'Pay no attention to Eden here; she's away with the fairies ... as stupid as her scatter-brained mother.' Both wine and emotion freed his tongue. 'And you can get off my property, Hezzle. You outstayed your welcome a long time ago.'

Eden squared up. 'Curtis, you're the most arrogant man I've ever met. You think you know everything; in reality you're as narrow-minded and as prejudiced as they come.'

'That does it. Eden, I'll drive you to the station.'

'In that state? You're drunk.'

'Drunk? You little bitch.'

Heather squealed. 'Something ran by the window.'

Curtis glared at the man. 'His dog I suppose.'

'No ...' Heather turned to Mr Hezzle, her eyes huge with fear. 'Mr Hezzle, what was it?'

But Eden answered first, 'The First Man. That's right isn't it, Mr Hezzle?'

Heather gave a pained grunt. Her eyes stayed locked on Eden's face as if she'd just screamed a blasphemy.

Curtis shook his head. 'Here we go ...' He grabbed

the bottle from the table and poured himself another massive glass of red wine while muttering, 'Welcome to the mad house.'

Eden approached the window. The garden lay empty beneath violent skies. Thunder bellowed again, fists of sound against her ears. 'I'm right, aren't I, Mr Hezzle?' She spoke with a new self-assurance. 'The First Man is out there. Does he bring the Gift?'

Her Aunt's voice rose. 'We identified those bones as *Homo Prima*, the First Man. The deformed skull.' She gave an odd-sounding laugh. 'How can that be the First Man out there. He'd have to be nearly two thousand years old?'

'The girl's an idiot.' Curtis' attention was on his wine glass and he took a large gulp of the merlot.

Mr Hezzle's wise eyes regarded Curtis with nothing less than pity. 'You should listen to your niece, Mr Laird. She is intelligent.' He sighed. 'More intelligent than the pair of you put together.'

A huge crash of thunder rattled the house. On the shelf the crockery trembled. Curtis chuckled and gestured with his glass. 'Take her to live with you, then. But be careful who she brings home for a one night stand. Her lovers have a reputation for starting fires. She'll bed the –'

He didn't finish the sentence. Eden snatched the glass from his hand then dashed its contents at his head. Blood red wine streamed down his face and dripped from his nose.

'Good work, Miss.' Mr Hezzle nodded with approval. 'It might wake him up enough to open his eyes properly for the first time.'

'I've never hit a woman before –' Curtis began ominously.

'Why don't you make the effort to see yourself as other people do?' Eden told him in contempt. 'No wonder Wayne slapped you.'

'I'm warning you!' He screamed the words. 'You and Hezzle have gone too far.'

Eden paused as she realised a vital truth. 'I know what's got into you. You aren't angry, Curtis. You're scared.'

'Rubbish.'

'You're frightened of what's out there.'

'No.'

'Listen to your niece,' Mr Hezzle said in a low voice. 'Like I said, she's intelligent. She knows.'

'Ridiculous ... I'm not frightened. She knows nothing.'

Eden's confidence grew. 'Curtis you are frightened. Because you've got a secret, haven't you?'

He looked at her, his mouth opening and closing as if he was lost for what to say next.

'There have been times at night,' Eden continued, 'when the moon is shining ... you've seen a figure moving through the fields. You watched and not told a living soul. But you saw a man. You noticed the shape of his head ... it didn't look right to you ... only you didn't tell anyone, did you?'

Curtis's appearance was that of a hunted man. His eyes became shifty as if he searched for an escape route.

Heather stiffened, 'Curtis, is this true?'

Eden said, 'That's why he doesn't like the house; he rationalises it as Dog Lands being too far from the studio in York. And that's why he drinks too much. He wants to sleep so soundly that he never gets up during the night to look out of the window to see what might be out there.'

Curtis swallowed and rubbed his face with his hand, smearing away the wine.

'Listen to your niece, Mrs Laird. What she says is true.'

'Of course it's true,' Eden lifted her voice above another rumble of thunder. 'What's made it all worse for Curtis is that I've given a name to the figure he's glimpsed in the fields. The First Man. What's more, he now has a history. He was revered by the Romans. He had a mission. Now he's returned to complete that mission. To offer humankind the Gift. Heather, it might seem contradictory, but the fact of the matter is the bones of the First Man are in the lab, yet the First Man is out there in the garden; he's searching for a way into the house.'

Curtis flinched, and his eyes shot to the bolted door.

Eden leaned forward to peer through the kitchen window. Winds tugged garden bushes. The gazebo that covered the pit had toppled. The storm was almost here. Another huge crash of thunder echoed around.

Heather gripped Eden's elbow. 'But how can this thing both be in the house as bones, and outside as a living creature?'

Eden glanced at Mr Hezzle, an invitation to supply the answer.

'You've done a good job so far, Miss. You tell her.'

Eden nodded. 'Because the First Man wasn't a single individual. I've been working it out. He didn't suffer from a deformity of the skull. He was completely normal. At least as far as his own species is concerned he was. As I say, the First Man isn't a solitary person. There was a group of males living here on this very spot.'

'What?' Heather looked on the verge of fainting.

Curtis plumped down onto a chair.

'They were from a race of hominids – those ancestors of ours that were referred to as "ape men". But they weren't especially ape-like. They'd just evolved differently to *Homo sapiens*. As their numbers dwindled they interbred with the local people. Look at Mr Hezzle. The structure of his nose is different to ours. Now, other people would rudely comment that he's got a considerable nose. But look at the shape of it. Notice his eyes. The bones beneath the eyebrows are more prominent. Yet his jaw line is extremely fine. Almost delicate. While just outside is one of the First Men.'

Heather asked in a weak voice, 'Mr Hezzle, is this true?'

He nodded. 'Out there is the last of his line. He can smell the bones.' The old man turned to face the direction of the lab. 'Something in me can, too.' His nostrils flared as he inhaled. 'It's like the skeleton is calling to us … a cry through the years.' His eyes watered. 'In a way I can't properly describe, I hate it. That cry is terrible … it's full of hurting, so full it makes me hurt, too, inside … but it makes me want to answer the call.' He regarded the three of them, his face grave. 'Rationally, I know it's coming from him outside. Yet he has this way of making his voice appear from other things … like from those bones. Sometimes when he calls, it comes out of the fields, out of the air, or even out of a storm like this. And he can plant ideas inside your head. Sometimes you dream *his* dreams. You find yourself knowing certain facts about him, about his history here over the last two thousand years or more, and you wonder how you could possibly have learnt all that information. That's his doing again. He has the power to feed knowledge directly into your brain. How does he do this? I can't rightly say. But he's got some telepathic way of making you know what he knows ... only it's disordered ... random ... it can seem as if there's a madness starting inside of you.'

He paused, and the first flicker of lightning lit the windows, throwing them all into stark relief before a huge clap of thunder rolled around the lowering skies.

Curtis attempted to sound like his old angry self. He picked up the two parts of the skull; the First Man's. 'Does it come out of these? The voices? Those fabulous airy-fairy notions!' He banged them down onto the kitchen table.

The second he did so, a shape hurled itself from the green gloom outside to slam against the back door. Through white fragments of shattered glass, held in place by the plastic membrane, all they could make out was a shape – a dark, angry shape driven by pure rage. The door jerked on its hinges. Heather screamed. Even Mr Hezzle flinched. Frightened into submission, Curtis gasped, 'My God,' and with shaking hands managed to pour himself another glass of wine. The figure charged the door again. It held ... just.

Eden hurried to the table.

'He wants this!' She picked up the sections of skull.

'Miss, you don't know everything about him. Even though he might have been feeding information into your head. There are dangers –'

'I do know that the First Men were the kindest and wisest men in the world. Your ancestors knew it; the Romans recognised them for what they were. The First Men were identified as having the entire pantheon of gods dwelling inside of them. What's more, he's been entrusting his knowledge to me without me ever realising it. Ever since I came here, I've had the strangest dreams. My mind began to work in a way that it's never done before. I understand so much about him without being told.' Eden smiled, her face growing rapturous. 'Can you imagine the impact of the First Man on the human race? He can elevate humankind into a new species – one that will have a longer life … no, more than that: *a better quality of life*. Now, the last one is outside. He's here to deliver the Gift'

Curtis trembled. 'What's she talking about?'

'Curtis. Thousands of years ago ancient people realised that if they interbred with the species of man-like creatures known at the First Men the children produced by that union would be more intelligent, highly resistant to disease, and have much longer life-spans. They realised that together they could produce a superior breed of humans.'

Mr Hezzle waited anxiously for a moment, expecting another violent assault on the door again. When the creature didn't return he pulled out a chair. 'Mr Laird. Sit down, please. There are things I have to tell you. This notion of interbreeding two species goes back two thousand years. Even now it would be considered revolutionary – nay, utterly terrifying to the outside world. That's why down through the centuries the villagers kept the existence of the First Men a secret. And that *Homo sapien* women were bearing the children of the First Men. Here we are, in a little Yorkshire village, creating a race of super humans simply by making love. Yes, indeed, children were born. They enjoyed long life-spans, their intelligence was higher. When bubonic plague swept the country, or there were outbreaks of cholera or smallpox those cross-bred individuals were immune. I'm one of the few remaining products of that particular experiment. I'm one hundred years old. I've never had so much as a common cold. And I daresay I could complete *The Times* crossword a sight faster than anyone here. However, we were fearful in Dog Lands. We knew that in centuries gone by the Church would have exterminated us if they discovered a new species of Man living in their midst. We'd be condemned as abominations. The Devil's bastards. That fear also resulted in us being extremely reluctant to move out of the area. We stayed put in Dog Lands for generation after generation. Consequently, a small gene pool resulted in inbreeding, which led to such a low fertility rate that by today our brave new race of men has dwindled to half a dozen geriatrics, myself included. So you see, our great world-changing experiment has failed. And failed woefully.'

'In that case,' Eden said, 'we should invite somebody else to join this debate.' With a thrill of excitement she crossed the kitchen. 'And he wants his kinsman's skull.'

Eden threw the top bolt open.

Mr Hezzle flinched. 'No, whatever you do, don't open that door!'

The lower bolt was removed and Eden turned and looked at them, a look of triumph on her face before she raced outside into the whirl of storm winds. Thunder pounded the house. She smelt electricity in the air. A wild, savage force that promised violent death in its touch.

15
Friday Night: 9.30

Eden ran in search of the First Man, the primeval creature, who might be the last of his kind. In her hand she held the two pieces of skull. A welcome gift. Then she'd learn wisdom from the one whom the Romans called Theopolis, the city of the gods. At that instant a shadow sped through the garden gate in the direction of the dyke. The water gleamed there in the deep, straight channel like liquid metal. The colour of lead. The essence of a dull reality, waiting to be transmuted by alchemy into something higher and ineffably golden. The First Man could work a unique change on the body. He'd transform a humanity limited by its mortality and restricted intellect into men and women with minds as precious as gold.

Mr Hezzle pursued her. He shouted warnings as she raced along the side of the water-filled dyke. Yet a giddy elation gripped Eden. She couldn't stop chasing that swift figure if she'd tried. Thoughts of miracles to come intoxicated. Marvellous possibilities whirled through her head. Excitement made her blaze within.

Stars burned in her blood; anything was possible in the next five minutes. Anything. Anything. Anything …

… Eden glimpsed fish gliding through the water of the dyke. Her mind appeared to swim like those creatures through a different medium altogether. The First Father had begun to exert his own particular magic. She remembered Mr Hezzle claiming that the First Father could reach into your head. That he could pipe his own memories, his own dreams, directly into one's unconscious mind. The water channel ran away into the distance, straight as an airport runway. Twenty feet wide, ten feet deep. Centuries ago it had been etched deep into the face of this land to drain swamp water.

'Eden, stop!' Mr Hezzle cried.

But she couldn't stop. Waves of emotion rolled through her. The urge to run as fast as she could after the shadow had her in a grip so muscular she gasped with something that merged pain with ecstasy. Her thigh muscles ached, pains shot through her feet, but there was a sweetness to it. This sweet pain felt so good after confinement in her aunt's house. *This is good; this is beautiful; this is release.*

Ahead, the shadow figure effortlessly sped through lush grass. It enticed her to an extraordinary destination; she knew that. Thunder clouted her ears. It shook the earth. Pregnant-looking clouds: swollen, huge, overwhelming, soon to break with waters unimaginable… how they'd sweep this flat land. A realm of fields, ditches, fences, solitary farmsteads, lonely trees, and, in the distance, the church ruin: clumps of masonry formed hunched goblin forms in the centre of the graveyard.

Eden ran faster, terrified lest the mysterious figure should slip away. *If only I could see you properly … You reached out to me. You filled my mind with new worlds of thought. Now I want to look into your face ...* Yet the gloom of the impending storm still hid him from her. He was shadow – that's all. Shadow, movement, a distant, half-glimpsed figure. 'Wait ... please wait ... I've got something for you ...' She held up the sections of skull. The thick, bony bulge of the brow above an eye socket pressed against the sensitive skin of her palm. *'Stop.'*

Emotion rolled through her with same power of the thunder now pounding the earth into submission. Longing, hope, yearning, excitement, terror, pain, exhaustion, exhilaration – each one vied for supremacy within her; each one triumphing for domination of her soul before being usurped in a near instant. Hope, terror, longing, dread, elation: they pulsed. The flow of sensations made her dizzy. At times she wondered if she'd fallen into a strange kind of sleep as she ran. The dimensions of the world were shifting. Grass blades swelled beneath her running feet. They expanded until they were as thick and as green as cucumbers. The clouds seemed to reach down to run cold fingers through her hair; she felt their icy touch on her scalp. The figure in front of her grew elongated ... now it seemed a hundred feet tall. Odd lights burned in its limbs. As if within that body it contained stars won from the heavens. Fragments of memory skittered through her. For a moment, it seemed none of this had ever happened. Eden Page rode the train again, the smell of the fire at home still in her nostrils. When could the builder start work? Would the insurance payout cover the cost of the entire kitchen? The turbaned man in the carriage solemnly intoned, *You should always respect omens ... beware, beware, beware ...* Then she was up to her shoulders in the pit in her aunt's garden. Scooping out bowls of mud. She stood in the grave of one of those creatures. Molecules of decayed flesh, mixed with fertile mud, stuck to her bare hands. Strong odours of burning, wet soil, damp grass, old wine ... And that's when the alchemy occurred. Nothing less than revelation blazed through the fibres of her being. Her old life, the job in the student lettings office, the apartment in a drab quarter of town, the sequence of fleeting love affairs, and the unfulfilling routines of the past were all meaningless. Quite frankly – all of it bloody pointless. Being here at this moment in time – that's what was important. Because being here in this muddy stretch of rural England went beyond the profound, the monumental and the momentous. Simply, she was poised to be present at the birth of a new world. A time as pivotal as when a primordial ape-creature struck two stones together to make fire. Or uttered the first word of rational speech.

Eden Page vaulted over a fence. The water in the dyke was rising up. Soon it would overflow. Would those lead-hued waters engulf her? Was her destiny to drown here? No she mustn't let that happen. Already her life had become woven with that of the individual she now so desperately followed.

Mr Hezzle's words came to her from when he spoke about the First Man in the kitchen just minutes ago: *'Yet he has this way of making his voice appear from other things ... like from those bones. Sometimes when he calls, it comes out of the fields, out of the air, or even out of a storm like this.'*

These waves of emotion ... the way the world around her had become distorted ... how grass stems became plump and bloated ... how far off things became near: the ruined church lay a mile away yet she saw its ruins suddenly magnified; the mad profusion of ivy that penetrated cracks in the stones; she saw graves ... the hardened soil split open with the ease of breaking apart freshly baked pies ... oh, but what kind of fruit lay inside ... what fillings ... what flavours? Did the First Man really feed those notions into her head? Was he truly responsible for changing how she perceived the world? Had he reached out a mysterious, unseen hand and touched her soul? Eden gasped – a sense of wonder that merged with utter terror erupted inside of her.

Eden didn't realise when it first happened but she'd fallen. She lay sprawling amongst thick grass that swarmed over her like vines. Her heart pounded. The water in the dyke rose. In that dark liquidity were shapes. Panting, she stared at what drifted there by the dozen. They were pear-shaped vessels ... no, it's more than that ... they were like inflated balloons. Completely transparent. A liquid as black as gloss paint filled those sacs. Through the membrane she glimpsed moving things. *I've seen those before. Back when I had that attack of vertigo in the excavation pit. Even then the First Man must have been showing me visions of the future. He needs me ...*

And when she looked, from where she lay at the edge of the watercourse, looked while the storm winds tore and rippled the grass, looked as her mind spun wildly on twin streams of horror and fascination, she saw what moved and twisted and pulsated and lived inside the tightly stretched membrane. Inside the transparent eggs, each the size of a beach ball, were figures. The glossy, black liquid washed over the naked bodies, but she discerned baby-like forms, with small arms and legs, yet possessing heads with adult faces. From smeared faces pairs of bright, intelligent eyes gazed through the membrane at her. The current in the dyke carried the shapes downstream. More rose to the surface to present their homunculus cargo to the light of that stormy day before slipping away. The urge gripped her to leap into the water to retrieve those inflated balloons. In her mind's eye, she saw herself swimming to the bank with one, then tearing open the sac – the black liquid would gush out over her hands – that done, she'd draw out the tiny figure, wipe the black stuff from its face with handfuls of grass then –

'Miss!'

An iron grip prevented her from leaping into the dyke. Dazed, she turned to see the man there. His prominent nose almost touched hers as he eased her from the water's edge.

'Don't go in. The banks are too steep. You'd never climb out again.'

'But I've got to save them ... they're being washed away ...'

'Save what, Miss?' Mr Hezzle kept a grip on her arm.

'The First Man must have made them ... they're like babies, but have the faces of fully grown adults ...'

'Remember, what I told you, Miss? Back at the house? About what he can do? He has strange thoughts. Somehow he makes them come out of objects; for instance, sometimes it's from out of a tree, or the ruins of that church over there. It can seem as if the trees or the walls talk to you, or they look like other things; it can make you feel as if your heart will burst with excitement. Or terror.'

'I saw them. Little men in transparent bags with something like black oil; as if they were in wombs ... they floated down that ...' She regarded the dyke. 'They *were* there.'

Water reflected a grey sky. The stream tugged at strands of green weed; nothing else.

'He made me see them?' she asked.

'He does that to others, too. And me. I heard a call come from your aunt's house … from those bones … but they're dead like any bones found in the earth. There's nothing special about them, any more than the bones of a dead king or a scientist or an artist are any more special than the bones inside us both. But he made me hear the bones call my name. I lay awake at night … all the time I could hear them crying. It gets so you're excited by the sound – as well as scared.'

She began walking. The shadow figure was far away now. 'I want to talk to him.'

'No.'

'But we'll lose him.'

Mr Hezzle sighed. 'You're a brave one, I'll give you that. You've got guts. Nearly everyone I've ever seen, who got anywhere near him, turned and fled. They couldn't cope with his effect on them. They panicked. I've seen grown men jump into that dyke just to get away. More than one poor wretch has drowned doing that.'

'I'm not frightened of him,' Eden said with conviction. 'I've been reading about the First Man. What's more, he's reached out to me. Mind to mind. Just as you say he can. I figured out what he is. The Gift will transform our lives.'

'I was right. You are intelligent. But you don't know everything about him.'

'He belongs to a different race of humans?'

'Yes.'

'He's the last of his kind?'

'That, too.' Mr Hezzle released her arm as he

realised she'd regained her senses.

'So, I need to talk to him.'

'He won't talk, Miss. He can't.'

This gave her pause. 'Why?'

'Eighteen hundred years ago: there were just two of the First Men left. Brothers. That's the elder of the pair.' He nodded at the part-burned bone in her hand. 'The younger brother knew he'd be the last one. He knew other things, too ...' Raindrops hit the grass. 'Miss, we're going to get soaked if we stand out here. Come back to your aunt's house. I'll explain there.'

'No. Tell me now.'

He shrugged. 'If that's what you wish.' Thunder rumbled. Across the fields a blue vein of lightning burned bright against black cloud. 'But you'll get only the basics of it. It's not safe to be outdoors. When the land is flat like it is here it turns people into targets for lighting. Not many trees, you see.'

She cast yearning eyes along the path; the shadow figure had gone. Eden ached to meet him. 'The figure we saw today, was that the younger brother?'

'That it is. Eighteen centuries ago, both knew that their time was nearly up. They lived in a thatched hut just where Dog Star House is now. Inside their bodies was the seed that would transform us *Homo sapiens*, into a species that would be as wise as them. The things they could do. They could heal the sick. They drained marshes. They knew how to farm the land better than anyone. And to smelt new kinds of metals that never rusted.'

'What else?'

Lightning flashed closer, and a crack of thunder broke overhead. 'I said that you'd get the short history. You might not fear this kind of weather.' He turned up his collar. 'I do. See that? Lying in the field over there?' He nodded at a pale blob in a far-off meadow. 'A cow. Just this minute she got struck by lightning. She'll have been dead before she hit the muck.' Rain fell harder. 'Come back to the house, miss.'

'No.'

'Don't think of trying to find him. You won't. Unless he wants to be found, then you'll wish you hadn't.'

'Something happened to him, didn't it?'

He nodded. 'This is it. The short version. Then I'm going whether you come or not. The two brothers were the last of their species. They lived long lives. Longer than any of us. But then the older of the brothers started to fail. He might have been a hundred years old or a thousand years old. Nobody really knew. So he decided his younger brother must be the keeper of the Gift. They worked together to change the brother's biology. Whether it was through thought, or by drugs they concocted, nobody knows. To all intents, however, he became immortal. He'd live for as long as it took for human beings to understand his teachings and for him to father enough children to start a new race of human beings.' He shuddered as the storm grew closer. 'You know, we might assume that if the body doesn't age the mind wouldn't age with it. But when the brother died, and my ancestors buried him, the last of the First Men suffered the solitude. He spoke to us, but didn't relate to us in the same way as he could with his brother. So although his body never aged, his mind did. Ultimately, he was flesh and blood. Imagine his life: He'd find love with a woman; there were children. I'm one of the descendents. Of course, he would live forever. The human woman inevitably grew old and died. He took other wives. But each time, of course, they aged ... they died ... they were mortal. The First Man grieved. It reached a point where he couldn't bring himself to make friends or to take another wife. Although his children were long-lived eventually sheer old age took them. He and only he was immortal. For some reason, he couldn't, or wouldn't, repeat the process on others that gave him such longevity. He didn't age. He didn't get ill. Generations in this village came and went; he retreated from life. How long it took I don't know. It might have been a thousand years after he watched the first Romans approach his house and recognise him for what he was, but at last his mind gave out.' He shrugged. 'My grandmother said even though his body couldn't die of grief his mind did. The thinking part of him, the part that reasoned, and remembered, and knew who he was, just evaporated. It left behind a brain with animal instincts only. As far as I know, he hasn't talked to anyone in generations, or even uttered a single word.' Mr Hezzle sadly shook his head. 'See that horse in the field over there? Now the First Man is as intelligent as him. Like a beast he gets hungry, gets tired, gets angry – that's all. Are you sure you won't go back home now, Miss? We'll catch our deaths.'

'But where does he live? Somebody cares for him, surely?'

'He keeps to the fields, sleeps in ditches; often he can't be found at all. There are some of us who think he goes underground into tunnels. We don't know where, though. Nobody's found so much as a cave round here.'

'How many know about the First Man?'

'Apart from one or two old folks in the village just us – the Hezzles.'

'So you're his keeper?'

'If you want to put it like that. Miss, please go home. The lightning's getting closer. You don't know how dangerous it is to be exposed like this.' As if to illustrate the point, the storm delivered a lightning bolt that shattered a tree at the other side of the dyke. The branches burst into flame.

'So what now? If you know the secret of the Gift. When are you going to share it with humanity?'

'I'm sorry, Miss. I can't stay here. It's not just me I'm frightened for. I'm probably the only one who can stop him breaking into the world out there.' Mr Hezzle flung his arm out as if to encompass Britain's cities, and beyond. 'He doesn't know right from wrong anymore. When he gets angry he hurts people.'

'Then you should tell the world about him. He'll help us all become better people.'

However, the old man turned and hurried in the direction of Dog Star House. He called back, 'Please. It's not safe. The storm's right on top of us.'

They moved quickly along the bank. Heavy rain drops pounded at their heads. The once placid surface of the dyke shivered as rain struck it. More than once Eden expected to see those sacs floating there that contained the tiny men and women, with bright watchful eyes. Not that there was anything now; had she imagined them? Through veils of rain the house emerged.

Mr Hezzle slowed. 'Is that smoke?'

Eden paused. No doubt about it. Smoke streamed from the roof. 'Mr Hezzle, did you see lightning strike the house?'

'No, but it's possible.' He stared as a flickering yellow glow manifested itself through a window. 'Can you see your family?'

'They must still be inside the house!'

They started to run along the bank of the dyke, and became aware of another sound. A rushing noise; a huge hissing – something that had the power to make the thunder seem small in comparison.

Mr Hezzle had just had time to shout, 'He's coming! He knows the bones are in the house! He's seen they're going to be burnt again!'

Eden looked back as a terrific blast of air struck them. A figure sped toward her; a bewildering tumult of shadowy limbs; a sense of a solid object moving so fast it couldn't properly be seen. Only eyes. They blazed like the headlamps on a car. A suggestion of utter rage pierced her brain. Then the air it drove before itself with such force intensified to the point it bowled her through the long grass, as if she was nothing more than a doll. Then the figure was past them and gone.

Dragging herself to her feet, she dashed toward the house. 'Come on, Mr Hezzle. I need you!' The man appeared astonished by her resilience, yet he scrambled to his feet to run after her. *A man of one hundred shouldn't be able to run that fast, heck he shouldn't be able to run at all,* she told herself, *but inside Mr Hezzle, isn't there human blood mixed with that of the First Man?*

They reached the garden gate. Mr Hezzle effortlessly maintained the same punishing pace as Eden. By now, smoke bled through the roof tiles of the house. Grey fumes vied with the rain for the control of the airspace.

Once through the gate into the garden, Eden saw that the back door had been ripped from its hinges and was resting at the far side of the lawn. He – the primordial hominid, the First Man, would-be begetter of a new race – had torn away the door, then flung it carelessly behind him.

What she said next was *utterly* unnecessary, but somehow *utterly* essential to voice: 'He's got inside!'

'No, Miss, let me go first.'

His plea went unheeded as she sped through the raw, gaping wound of the doorway, its torn frame hanging in pieces; even the surrounding brickwork had been shattered by the force of entry.

'It's me, Eden Page,' she shouted as she moved through the kitchen. 'I'm here. Don't worry. You're safe.' *I'm not talking to Heather and Curtis,* she thought in surprise. *I'm talking to* him.

She found herself engulfed in thick smoke, her arms sweeping before her, as she felt a route through the burning building. After the coldness of the rain the hot air against her face became searing. Its heat dried her clothes in seconds. In the hallway mirror she glimpsed herself through roiling fumes. Her hair steamed. Yet her eyes were bright, alive, eager – disconcertingly eager.

'Don't be afraid. I'm here to help you.'

She pushed open the living-room door. There a figure pounced on her.

In the smoke filled room all she could make out were two hands that gripped her throat. Then a voice.

A familiar voice: 'I should have done this days ago! I'm burning the bloody bones! Did you hear, you idiot girl? Humpty's bones – they're going up in smoke!'

'Curtis. You've got to get out.'

Another hand reached up from the floor to grip her thigh. 'Curtis has set fire to the house.' Heather couldn't manage to rise from the living room floor. She coughed, desperately trying to draw air in the smoke-filled room. 'He threatened to do it before … I warned you not to frighten him.'

'Curtis. Let me take Heather outside. The smoke's

killing her.'

'No, we're staying … we're staying. We're going to watch those blasted bones turn to ash.'

There was a thud from elsewhere in the house and his face changed. 'Where is it? I know it got inside.'

Mr Hezzle stood in the doorway trying to catch his breath, the thick smoke was choking him. 'He's in the room with the bones. He's trying to save them.'

'Get it out!' screamed Curtis. 'Get it out of my home!'

He lunged at Mr Hezzle, pushing him down. Disorientated by terror and smoke he grabbed the ornate walking stick from the stand in the hall then rushed down to corridor to the lab where the bones were kept – and the smoke was thickest. For one panic-driven moment he made one last attempt to tackle the figure that had broken into his house. He shouted hoarsely and waved the stick through the smoke. But his fragile courage only lasted a split-second. With a high pitched shout his nerve broke. He turned and blundered down the corridor, away from the lab. Eden tried to stop Curtis from hurting himself as he crashed against the walls, sending pictures flying and ornaments crashing to the floor in his desperation to escape.

'No! No! Let go of me!' Sweat poured down his face. His eyes blazed in pure fear. 'Don't let it touch me. For God's sake! Let go.' He pushed by, then scrambled out of the house, screeching like an injured pig.

'Mr Hezzle.' Eden made her way to where the man was slumped. She helped him up. 'Get my aunt out of here. The smoke's killing her.'

He seemed uncertain on his feet, so Eden went into the living-room, pulled her aunt upright, then made sure the pair supported each other as they moved unsteadily toward the back door.

Mr Hezzle coughed, his eyes were streaming; nevertheless, he called back, 'Miss? Where are you going?'

'I'm going to help him save the bones.'

He gave her a look that said all too clearly: *Please don't. Save yourself.* But he knew the strength of her spirit now.

16
Friday Night: 10.30

When Eden Page moved toward the lab it seemed as if she crossed a threshold. She passed from this reality of the house, one that burned because Curtis's mind had snapped, to enter another reality; one that seemed misty rather than smoke-filled. The house became strangely quiet. When she stepped through the doorway into the room that contained the skeleton she saw a pool of burning petrol on the floor. Its brightness equalled a noonday sun in the breathless zenith of summer. A desperate figure strode back and forth. It longed to save the skeleton on the burning table; only its animal mind couldn't tell it how. Instead it pounded its bare chest with the flat of one hand, while running its fingers through its hair with the other. She'd expected to find a heavy ape face – a kind of muscular gorilla visage; all black fur, thick curling lips, yellowing fangs. Instead, she saw a fine-boned face of immense delicacy. No facial hair; the teeth shone white. From that face a pair of wise yet wounded eyes were held by the spectacle of bones beginning to char on the table.

'Let me help,' she found herself saying in a gentle voice. 'We'll put the bones into this bag.' She pulled a canvas sack from a shelf. Ancient pottery fragments began to pop with the heat. Eden extended her hand to take a thigh bone.

With a cry the First Man pushed her hand away. His fingers were long, tapering, the kind of fingers she'd expect belonging to a musician. Despite the way he'd torn away the house door from its frame, he wasn't stockily built. The name First Man had prepared her for an ancient creature but this was a man in his youth. His face had a smoothness of a sculpted Apollo. His naked skin was clean; the hair on his head shone with health. True, his nose and brow were the dominant features of his face. However, there was nothing ugly or beastlike; instead he resembled one of those graceful statues found in museums; of beautiful youths in pure white marble that are eternally waiting for the gods to breathe life into their still bodies.

The heat reached a shelf of chemicals that Heather used to preserve her finds. Blue fire belched out across the ceiling. The First Man didn't flinch. He needed to save the bones of his brother.

That's all that mattered.

All he cared about.

His mind had gone, true, but an old love still endured.

Eden once more reached out to the bones. 'I won't damage them. I'm helping,' she said firmly yet gently. 'I know about you. I know that you won't hurt me. You are good and wise.'

He watched her move the bones from the table to the bag. There was anxiety in his eyes. He tensed, as if at any moment he'd snatch the bones from her. But then he understood. This female stranger wasn't causing harm. She was rescuing sacred treasure from the flame. For the first time he raised his eyes so they locked with hers.

Eden moved automatically. Her hand glided across the table to gently transfer the bones into the bag. At that instant, it seemed as if she watched her actions from outside herself. There, in the burning room, stood a woman by the name of Eden Page. Her fingers were scorched by heat. Smoke formed a dense fog. Yet still the slight form of the woman worked to save the ancient bones. Her features were smooth, untroubled, almost relaxed. And standing at the other side of the table, a tall figure. A man who had carefully husbanded his Gift for eighteen hundred years. A remarkable man, the last of his species, and possibly the first of another.

Eden placed the remaining skull fragments in the bag. Her mind floated free of its flesh now. It seemed as if she passed into a coma as she stood there. A drowsiness seeped through her veins to feed shadows into her head. Ancient vases exploded before the intense heat. Hot air currents made her hair stream upward. Yet Eden only heard the beat of her heart; her skin felt cool. The First Man stepped through the barrier of smoke. He reached out slender fingers to touch her face. A sensation of taking a cold, refreshing drink on a hot day passed through her; a thirst quenching draught. Instead of smoke, she smelt dew on a spring lawn. Then Eden had a vision of this man – this young-old being. Perhaps what she saw had actually happened, and he poured his own memories into her brain in a way she didn't understand. The vision revealed images of the First Man and his kind living here in houses made of turf and thatch five thousand years ago. Then refugees reached here after being driven out of their homeland by tribal wars. The First Men welcomed the exhausted people that carried their starving children. They gave the refugees food, shelter and so much more. Then she saw the winter's day when Roman soldiers marched along the newly built *Via Britannicus* to their provincial garrisons. A brutally cold morning, when Hezzle's ancestors hacked open the frozen earth to lay something withered, yet still glorious into the ground. The last of the First Men sang with his neighbours as men refilled the grave. That cleft in the soil would never be completely sealed, however. It would receive gifts of coins for the next eighteen centuries. The walls of the house began to flow. Eden realised arms supported her; the First Man carried her out of the burning house. Cool rain soothed her scorched body. The sky was a tumult of black, green, grey and blue.

They went to the pit at the bottom of the garden. After tenderly placing his brother's bones back into the grave, The First Man carried Eden away. She glimpsed Heather and Curtis. Their faces were strangely blanched shapes, huddled together by the road, as they watched her departure. Mr Hezzle was there. He began to raise his hand to stop the First Man taking her. Then he dropped his arm, stood aside: he understood.

Waves of sleep washed over Eden as the man ran with her in his arms. At times fully conscious before slipping away once more. Dimly, as if the real world had become an unreal phantom, she glimpsed fields, fences, trees rushing by. The dyke overflowed. Instead of presenting formal straight lines, it had flooded out over the meadows to become a formless shape with careless, rounded edges. As her mind surrendered to unconsciousness she once again visualised the First Man's existence. The swift passage of lovers and sons and daughter from life to death. The repetition of meeting, bonding, then parting became too much for him. Grief accumulated. The weight of sadness became too much. As the centuries passed his upper-mind slipped away. The power of speech evaporated. Now he had the instincts of a fox.

When that instinct told him they were safe from the flames he set her down. They stood face to face in a far-flung heath. An empty place. No houses. Not so much as a single tree. Here, a vast blanket of grass rooted into wet dirt. Eden's feet sank into moist turf. Rain sighed from the heavens. The First Man closely watched her face as if he saw someone he half-remembered. Perhaps her expression was familiar, rather than her features. He could read a meaning there. An intention.

The effort of trying to remember grew too intense; he shuddered. At the same time he began to turn away. Instinct told him it was time to leave.

'No.' She forced that cloying drowsiness out of her mind. 'I want you to stay.'

She put her arms around him. The muscles in his back quivered at her touch.

'You remained here for a purpose. I'm going to help you remember.'

His eyes darted as if an inner voice urged him to escape.

'Stay,' she murmured. 'Stay.'

At last, he allowed his body to relax. He lay down on the ground, the spontaneous act of a creature needing to rest a while. She lay beside him. The wet grass drenched her; mud turned her fingers slippery as she moved so she could lie close to him. There, she gazed up into the dark cloud that spilled its rain onto their bodies.

When she spoke she addressed herself as much as the man: 'I have a purpose now. We're going to leave our mark on this world.'

It didn't happen straight away. By degrees, by subtle signs of acceptance, he allowed her to embrace him as they lay there. When his arms encircled her in a hug of such simple, yet heart-warming fondness, she had to gasp. She'd wanted this to happen. She absolutely did. But the realisation that she'd found a way through a defensive shell into his affection caught her by surprise. The knowledge he wanted her moved Eden.

'At last,' she murmured

.

Six Months Later

Eden Page wrote this e-mail:

Dear Heather,

Here are some photographs. I hope you like what I've done with the house. You'll see the kitchen is now in limed oak. The windows are twice the size they were; it's made the place very bright and airy. The fire didn't cause as much damage as first thought. I must add, Mr Hezzle and his family have been a great help. They really are wonderful neighbours. They've worked miracles.

It's good to hear that Uncle Curtis is well on the road to recovery. The both of you retiring to Portugal has been very wise. I'm sure the climate suits you perfectly.

Tell me what you think of the photographs of the rooms now they're finished. I think you'll be amused by the one entitled 'The Old Laboratory'. It's now my study. Dog Star House is a home again. I'm very content here.

Lots of love, Eden.

With the e-mail sent, Eden stepped out into the pleasant sunlight of an Autumn afternoon. A few apples remained on the trees in the orchard. They glowed red with a full ripeness. Beside one tree a slight dip in the ground marked where her aunt had excavated the grave. Now grass had grown over it. From time to time, people would take the old path from the village to stand by it for a while. Each visitor would drop a coin into a narrow cleft that formed something like the opening to a rabbit's burrow. Often they told Eden how pleased they were that she'd issued an invitation to practice their devotion whenever they wished.

Eden strolled to the back gate. The dyke, a narrow waterway as straight as a ruler, seemed to run through the fields into infinity. In the meadow Mr Hezzle drove his tractor. Cheerfully, he raised a hand in greeting. She waved back.

Content, relaxed, in love with her new life here at Dog Star House, she luxuriated in gazing out across this strangely beautiful, if forgotten realm of England. Eden's eye focused on the distant horizon where ploughed earth became married to blue sky. Eden wished she could see a certain figure racing through the sunlight toward her. But she knew that wouldn't happen by day.

He called on her at night. When all the shadows merged into one. When traffic absented itself from the *Via Britannicus*. When villagers closed the doors of their houses. Birds returned to their roosts. Cattle dozed in the pasture. That's when Eden Page would open the back door to find him standing there, his bright eyes fixed on hers.

Then he'd softly stroke her face and whisper, 'Eden loves'. In the past, his voice had appeared to emanate from everywhere but his lips. What's more, it had been a disordered stream of half-memory mixed with raw emotion. However, gradually, over the last few weeks he'd begun to speak to her. Albeit haltingly. Nevertheless: speech meant mind. Mind meant intelligence.

Many a time these lines would run through her head: *All the king's horses, and all the king's men, couldn't put Humpty together again.*

But she had.

A bird singing on the fence drew Eden back to the sunlit present. She smiled. The miracle had happened. For her, the changes in her body were quite plain to see. And her ancestors had provided her with the words to describe just what the result would be.

'Our child.'

And will that birth mean the end of Mankind as we know it? she mused. *Well only time, and Darwin's ghost, could tell ...*

DANGER SIGNS AND OTHER ALLUREMENTS

Introduction

Okay. You're aged twelve, or thereabouts. You're walking along a path when you see the sign: DANGER! KEEP OUT! Do you keep walking calmly forward, while praising the foresight of that considerate person who planted the sign that warns of untold hazards? Do you heck! If you're twelve DANGER! KEEP OUT! really means LOTS OF EXCITING STUFF HERE! COME ON IN!

And in you rush, eager for adventure. In English law, such a temptation that induces children to trespass into forbidden areas (where harm lurks) is known as an 'Allurement'. As you might imagine, lots of rather grim legal cases feature the word aplenty. When I was a child, roaming the fields near where I lived, a danger sign would elicit excited shouts from my friends. For example, we once defied DANGER OF FALLING MASONRY warnings to search for a secret tunnel that linked Rogerthorpe Manor with a hilltop known as Upton Beacon, a distance of two miles. Regrettably, the so-called secret tunnel only extended five paces into the back of some grotty outbuilding. Another foray into a forest that bristled with danger signs seemed quite dull until I heard one of my friends shouting 'Help! Help!' in a strangely strangled voice. Thinking he was mucking about, I pushed through thick bushes to find that they suddenly ended. Literally ended in thin air. The bushes formed a dense fringe along the top of a quarry. My friend hung onto a branch, his face distorted in terror, while his feet kicked fresh air some hundred feet above jagged rocks below.

Quickly, I hauled him back from the precipice, and the threat of instant death. On the way home we agreed it was an exciting day out, and we'd visit the quarry again soon.

All these childhood memories were bubbling away in the back of my head when I started to write this story. After all, childhood is a world where the laws of time, logic, perception and behaviour don't apply in the same way as they do in the adult world. Kids are drawn to derelict buildings (where bricks might fall on heads, or an individual might plunge through a rotten floor); kids love to mess around at the edge of deep ponds; they light campfires, then throw on canned beans to see what happens. Then some bright spark produces an aerosol (marked *highly flammable*) and asks the question, 'I wonder what'll happen if we put this on the fire?' My friend, Victor, emptied out the contents of a handful of fireworks, then applied a lit match to the mound of black granules. At school the next day we marvelled at what a boy looked like without eyebrows or hair (at least on the front half of his head). Most boys hurried home that night determined to repeat the exciting experiment.

So: to the story. What happens if a group of children walk by an old military base? They've been this way many times before. There are DANGER SIGNS, of course. High fences. Barbed wire. Sadly, for them, the big old concrete bunkers are securely locked up.

Then, one day, they notice that one of the massive steel doors to a bunker lies open. Beyond this yawning doorway a passageway leads into the mysterious heart of the building. The darkness within oozes excitement, it whispers to their imagination: *secrets lie inside*.

So: When you were twelve what would you do? The sensible option would be to tell yourself it's too dangerous to go anywhere near that once sealed up bunker.

Or would you take just a little peek inside?

Over the page, four children face that allurement. Just between you and me, I think they're going to take that little peek through the bunker doorway. First, though, they're going to climb through the fence that bears a sign.

The one that reads:

CAUTION!
RESTRICTED MILITARY ZONE
DO NOT PASS.
DANGER OF DEATH!

Simon Clark
Yorkshire
14 December, 2009

DANGER SIGNS

1

Pitt is twelve years old. Pitt is also crazy. Although it still shocked me when he told me what he planned to do.

'You're insane,' I told him. 'You don't know what's in there.'

'Probably a psycho,' said Jenny.

'Or poisonous chemicals.' Adam looked worried.

'And missiles full of flesh-eating virus.' I nodded at a sign on the fence. 'That's been put there for a reason.'

On the sign, this warning in big, shouting letters:

CAUTION!
RESTRICTED MILITARY ZONE
DO NOT PASS.
DANGER OF DEATH!

'That clear enough for you, Pitt? You go in there you're a dead man.'

He whirled round at me. 'Hey, Naz. Are you saying I'm scared? Do you think I'm frightened of that?' He punched the sign so hard it gave a heck of a clatter. Birds flew in panic from the trees. The notice was so old the painted side began to peel away from its wooden backing. The sign, itself, was a thin metal sheet. One still shiny enough to reflect the sunlight like hazard lights – as if to say: *Warning. Peril ahead.*

'No, I'm not saying you're a coward. But if there are danger signs ...'

'He's right,' Adam said, 'if you ignore warnings you're asking for trouble.'

Pitt snarled, 'I don't care about any stupid sign. I'm going in.'

With that he left without us. We watched him through the hole in the fence as he strolled in bright sunshine to the military bunker. The size of a house, it was built out of concrete that had been painted in camouflage greens. There were no windows. Only a big steel door. For the first time in our lives we saw the door was open. Wide open. Yawning so big it looked like a monster's mouth. Beyond the door lay a dark tunnel. Like I said, Pitt's crazy. But I didn't want him to go into the bunker. I'd got a bad feeling about that place.

Let me explain something before I go any further. Okay, even though Pitt acts crazy we've been friends for years. He's done things like put wings on his bike, rigged a motor to his skateboard (that got him a week off school with a twisted knee). When he talks about building a rocket we say he's crazy. Then, deep down, we respect his amazing plans.

Yesterday had been a bad day for Pitt. We'd been walking across the playing field into town. Who should turn up but Adam's fourteen year old brother, Brian, and his buddies. They'd been riding these illegal dirt bikes, revving the engines like lunatics. They'd ridden them close enough to make us dodge out of the way. Brian had made fun of Pitt for jumping 'like a frightened little kid'. Then Brian had ridden the bike across the grass like a bullet. He'd swung a sports bag into Pitt's face. It smacked him hard enough to cut his lip.

Adam had told his big brother to stop being a jerk. Brian laughed it off, saying Pitt shouldn't act so soft.

So today Pitt had turned up with this bashed mouth. The wound resembled a little red flower on his bottom lip. When he touched the cut with his finger it still oozed blood. It looked really sore. Every so often he flinched as if it stung like it was on fire.

There were four of us – Pitt, Jenny, Adam, and me, Naz. All twelve year olds. We tried to cheer up Pitt as we walked through the woods but you could tell the attack by Brian still bugged him. He'd got real anger in his eye.

When we saw what had happened to the bunker it made us forget everything else.

Pitt had stared in wonder. 'After all these years. That's the first time I've seen the door open.'

When he realised there was nobody about, that's when he announced he was going inside. So through the hole in the fence he went – ignoring the danger sign.

And that brings us to now – this very moment when Pitt wanted to prove to us that he was no coward. One second he stood in the open doorway then he vanished inside.

'His funeral,' Adam grunted.

'We can't just leave him,' Jenny protested. 'What happens if he gets hurt?'

I agreed. 'If he calls for help nobody will hear. It's a mile to the nearest house.'

Adam gazed at the sign – DANGER OF DEATH – like it would grow claws and rip off his head. 'They put that up for a reason. My uncle used to deliver propane here twenty years ago. He said they had nuclear weapons in underground tunnels.'

Jenny pointed at the bunker. 'Kids have covered the walls with graffiti. The army wouldn't have allowed that if it had still been in use.'

'Oh no. I know what you're going to do,' Adam was horror-struck. 'You're going in there, aren't you?'

This stopped me dead because I'd planned to wait here by the fence until Pitt returned. *And surely he'll come back soon. There's nothing in the bunker that could hurt him, was there?* Even so, that yawning doorway looked so darkly forbidding. Even the concrete bunker reminded me of a big dinosaur skull. From that grim building came a yell. Or was it a cry of pain?

'Jenny,' Adam caught hold of her arm. 'Wouldn't it be best to wait here?'

'Didn't you hear it? That shout came from Pitt. We've got to see if he's alright.' She gave us a hard stare. 'Well, I'm going in if you're not.'

I groaned. I'd no choice. I couldn't let her go in there alone. Quickly, I followed her to the bunker. That huge metal door, fully six inches thick, made me have worrying thoughts about the entrance to ancient tombs. A darkly forbidden place.

Jenny regarded it with awe. 'This door's huge.'

'It's bomb proof!'

'How could anyone have broken in here?'

Adam checked the entrance more closely. 'See these gouge marks on the inside of the door? The way it's scratched all over?' He gulped. 'Nobody's broken in here. *They've broken out.*'

2

This is frightening. We entered the bunker. There was no light at all. You know when you reach out of bed in the middle of the night to switch on the lamp? Even though you're alone, isn't there always that moment when you search for the switch that you fear you're going to touch some living body; something with cold skin; or with manky hair? Just imagine the shock. Your fingers suddenly feel a face with bulging eyes, and – *'Get it off me! It's biting!'* From the darkness came a yell of terror. 'There's something alive in here!'

'Adam –'

'Help me!'

'Shush, it's me.' Jenny shouted. 'I pushed your head down so you didn't bang it. There are chains hanging from the ceiling with hooks on them.'

'Hooks? What kind of hooks?' Adam still sounded frightened. 'I want out of here. It's too dark. There's something wrong about this place ...'

Even though the dark made me nervous I couldn't stop myself saying, 'And make sure you don't step on the snakes. They're everywhere. Sssss ...'

'Naz.' Jenny sounded annoyed. 'That's not helping.

Adam, there are no snakes.'

'It's the vampires you have to watch out for.'

'Naz.' Jenny's eyes must have adapted to the gloom enough to target me. I felt her fist thump my arm. 'Stop scaring Adam.'

'Didn't you hear me earlier?' Adam's voice wavered. 'There were no marks on the outside of the bunker door. It had been gouged on the *inside.* Nobody broke in here. Something broke *out.* And it must be *huge.*'

What he said made us fall silent. I pictured a big animal prowling down this passageway to bump aside the chains hanging from the ceiling before attacking the door – snarling, gouging, then battering it in total fury. A shiver ran down my spine.

I whispered. 'Maybe we should wait for Pitt outside?

Only it was too late for that. Far too late.

We were in the middle of that darkness. It seemed to drown us in deep, deep black. Then … a scraping noise. We flinched. Adam moaned in fear. 'Oh, man … *it knows we're here …'*

Slowly, a door creaked open, a strange door that worried the life out of me. Weird! It was as narrow as the lid of a coffin. A light shone through it as a ghostly figure stepped through the gap. Its face was a cold blue. It beckoned to us with these chilling words. *'You can't go back. You must come with me.'*

3

For what seemed like an age we froze. We stared at the figure. Stared as a blue light burned with a strange, phantom intensity. Stared as the weird apparition loomed through the doorway.

Adam pointed. *'Look, there's something wrong with its mouth.'*

For some reason I found my eyes yanked to those monster-size fishhooks that hung from chains above our heads and wondered if –

'Come on,' boomed the figure. 'You've got to look at this! I've been calling you for ages. Didn't you hear? Naz, what's wrong? You look as if you've stood on a ghost.'

'Pitt?' I blinked. 'Is that you?'

'Who do you think? Frankenstein?'

Jenny shook her head. 'The phrase, Pitt, is "seen a ghost" not "stood on one." '

'Whatever.'

Adam swayed. 'I was so scared I thought I'd puke … think I still am.'

The weird ghostly effect was caused by a blue light shining onto Pitt from the room that led off this corridor.

Of course, the 'something wrong with his mouth' comment by Adam referred to the scabby cut on his lip.

'Aw, come on, people.' Then this from Pitt gave me chills: 'When you see what I've found you're not going to believe your eyes.'

4

Adam lagged back in that corridor of chains. 'I'm not going. There's something bad about this place. Can't you feel it?'

'Trust me,' Pitt called as he clattered down a staircase. 'You'll remember this until the day you die!'

Jenny went through the door. I followed. Blue lamps lit the stairs making our skin glow strangely.

'Daylight bulbs,' Jenny explained. 'They're used in places where people stay indoors for months at a time.'

We ran down the steps after Pitt. Even so, I felt cold. As if instinct warned me danger lay ahead.

'Don't leave me alone!' Adam shouted. He realised that once the door swung shut he'd be alone in that dark corridor with its hooky chains.

A second later we pushed through big double doors into ... well ... I couldn't believe my eyes. I just stared.

Pitt whistled. 'Look at this. It's all twenty feet underground. And it doesn't smell like poop. There's air-conditioning.'

I struggled to take it all in. 'There's a kitchen. A lounge. Sofas. And is that a TV?'

'The screen's six feet wide,' breathed Jenny in awe. 'Look at all those DVDs.'

Adam walked in, gob-smacked. 'A house underground? How weird is this?'

Jenny said, 'Last year we went on a school trip to an old military bunker. It had stuff like this. Bedrooms, kitchens, offices. If there's a nuclear attack that's where all the generals would stay so they could run things. This one must be kept unmanned until there's an emergency.'

I checked out the DVDs. A lot were new movies. 'Maybe the government will stay down here if there's a war. When they aren't working they'd come here to relax.'

'We shouldn't be in here,' Adam said. 'We're trespassing.'

I shrugged, 'The door's open.'

'We could get into trouble.'

'Scared?' Pitt grinned. 'Let me take your mind off going to jail. Da-dah!' He swung open a fridge door. Packed with chocolate! Every shelf had neat stacks of chocolate in bright blue wrappers. Right at the front of the confectionary was a single bottle of tomato ketchup, with a dried dribble of sauce stuck to the label. He opened another door to reveal frozen chickens. 'People could live for months down here.'

Adam followed us in a daze. 'But that door upstairs? Something clawed at it. Then bust it open. What happens if it comes back?'

Only we were too excited exploring to listen to his warning. But we should have done. We really should. Because what happened next was the most terrifying thing I've ever experienced.

5

We'd discovered that the big TV had a games feature. Jenny and Pitt were figuring out how to get the two silver androids onscreen to shoot down the helicopter gunship when ...

'Hey guys.' Adam's eyes bulged in fear. 'Did anyone hear that?'

Pitt studied the onscreen *Game Help*. 'Hear what?'

'Bad news, guys. Someone's coming down the stairs!'

This time we froze.

'What if we're caught down here?' I whispered. 'It might be the police.'

'Or soldiers?'

Adam shuddered. 'Or the thing that smashed open the door.'

That complex of subterranean rooms had been brightly lit. But somehow the light seemed to fade. The bright greens and oranges of the furniture became dull. That big glassy TV screen seemed to resemble a huge alien eye. One that stared with hatred. Or so it seemed to me. A cold, cold sensation crept through my veins. For some reason a pain flared above my right eye. It must be

THAT SOUND. I'd heard nothing like it before. *Something was coming down the stairs we'd used just ten minutes ago.*

Jenny whispered, 'It doesn't sound like ordinary footsteps.'

A soft clump, clump. Shivers ran along my arms.

Pitt turned to face the stairway door. It was closed. Even so, he heard all too clearly. 'A voice … but can anyone hear what it's saying?'

'That's no human voice.' I heard a low snarling. Also, I made out words but not in a language I understood. *'Neefer-ratt-saaar.'*

'It's getting closer.'

The door began to creak open. *'Neefer-ratt-saaar.'*

'Run!'

'But where,' cried Adam. *'That's the only way out!'*

6

Panic! We searched for somewhere to hide. Jenny pointed to another door. 'Through there!'

A sign on it read *DANGER. NO ENTRY*. But this was no time to pause. Behind us the stairway door creaked. That strange, menacing voice grew louder: '*Neefer-ratt-saaar.*' After that, an excited snorting as if a hungry beast had smelt food. Beyond the door Jenny had pointed out were more steps – only these went down, deep underground. The stairwell was a gloomy pit, descending into a forbidden, dangerous place. Here were yet more signs. *CAUTION. NO ENTRY. DANGER OF DEATH!*

7

The four of us dashed downstairs. Upstairs, whatever had entered the bunker must be in the lounge. *Does it know we're here? Will it follow?*

'Sheesh,' Pitt gasped. 'What is this place?'

Jenny raced into a maze of tunnels. 'Keep moving. We don't know if that thing's going to come after us.'

'What we gotta do,' panted Adam, 'is find a way out. Fast!'

These tunnels were gloomy places. Shadows lurked at every corner. I guessed the tunnels were broad enough to accommodate three buses side-by-side, they were certainly high enough, too, but the length? They stretched faraway into the distance. And did I mention the cold? Breath misted out all white. In the tunnels were huge, hulking forms covered with plastic sheets. Adam was so frightened he hurried forward without pausing to look. Pitt hauled up the sheets.

'Hey, a Jeep. And check this out ... wow! A tank. Look at the size of that gun.'

Jenny whistled. 'This is where the army must keep spare equipment, just in case the other stuff gets wiped out in an attack.'

Pitt's eyes shone. 'I wonder if there are any rockets.'

Jenny started to say, 'You can forget taking –'

BANG!

Adam shouted, 'That's the door to the stairs – something just bashed it open.'

By now the entrance we'd come through was way off in the distance. Just a speck. But we could make out *another* speck. *This one moved.*

Fast!

'It's found us!'

We ran like crazy. By tanks, vans, troop carriers, all covered with sheets of plastic. They formed sinister mounds. They hinted at deathly things.

In the gloom, the confusion, the speed at which everything happened, it was inevitable. I turned off into another tunnel. A minute later I stopped to get my breath back. Then I saw the others weren't with me.

'Pitt, Jenny, Adam. Where are you?' There was no reply. A deadly silence filled the tunnel. My friends? No sign. Only the unnerving shapes of vehicles under grey shrouds. At any second that demon-thing might prowl round the corner. Here I was, alone.

All alone.

8

Listen. When you're alone, your head fills with thoughts, doesn't it? If you're walking by yourself through a forest you start to imagine you're being followed. If you're alone at night, then open the blind to look out, you're convinced a stranger's face will look back at you through the glass. Being alone can make your imagination turn bad.

There in the tunnel, deep underground, I waited. I could hear my own breathing. I saw warnings: *CAUTION. HAZARD ZONE.* At any moment I expected that monstrous thing to come roaring at me. But what was it? There was a sense of menace and strength about it, but I'd not seen it clearly. It had only been a speck at the far end of the tunnel. Just what could live down here that could break out through a thick bunker door?

Shivering, I continued walking in the hope I'd find another exit to the surface. Then a sight met my eyes that didn't give me any hope. One of the plastic sheets had been ripped to pieces. Shreds of grey covered the floor. A container on a truck had been broken open. Soldiers' helmets had tumbled out. I picked one up. There were four holes in it, big enough to wiggle my fingers through. Bite holes.

'They sure have big mice round here.' I tried to laugh at my own joke but the echo made me flinch. 'Time to get out of here, Naz,' I told myself. 'Otherwise you're going to end up as dinner.'

9

I went through the tunnel. Silence oppressed me. That quietness felt like a towel pressed over my face. At times, that alone, seemed as if it would stop me breathing. When I paused to catch my breath the silence got even worse. All I could hear was the scratchy rasp ... rasp as I breathed in and out. The air from my lungs blew in white blasts in the harsh light. Got to find the others, I told myself. Then gotta get out. Get away from here.

Because I knew the truth – down here we were not alone. Some *thing* hunted us. As I rested for a moment I looked back the way I'd come. I stared until my eyes watered. All those vehicles covered in grey plastic sheeting. They waited for war. Above me, on the tunnel roof, clung a big black object with spider legs. My eyes locked onto it. A gurgle sounded in my throat as my heart raced – bang, bang, bang. Then I took a deep breath. The spider object was some kind of mechanical hoist bolted to the ceiling. That's all. The black legs were a steel grab. Probably the soldiers used it to load equipment onto these trucks that lined the tunnel like slumbering beasts.

I rubbed my eyes then checked the tunnel again.

Nothing there ... yet. I continued walking. My footsteps echoed from the walls.

'Pitt, Jenny, Adam.' The call came as a whisper rather than a shout. A sense of danger filled me. I didn't dare shout the names of my friends, just in case *it* heard. I shuddered. Were they still safe? Or had they been caught? Dread oozed inside of me. What if I never saw the three again? What would I say to their parents? If the worst happened, who would tell the police? Imagine having to identify the bodies? I pictured figures lying under sheets on the ground. There'd be police dressed in those white forensic suits with the tight little hoods. One would start to pull back the sheet. 'Okay, son. This isn't going to be nice. Brace yourself for a shock. But take a good long look at what's left of the face ... and tell me the name of the person you see lying there.'

Suddenly, a whispering startled me. I'd been so preoccupied with imagining the gruesome scene with the police that I nearly leapt out of my skin. A grey shape began to swell outwards across the tunnel. I couldn't run back because I might bump into whatever followed me. Now I couldn't go forward because a grey, lumpy mass blocked my way.

'Idiot,' I panted. 'It's only the plastic sheeting.' I took a closer look. The relief! I even tingled with embarrassment when I realised what had happened. A ventilation duct at the other side of the truck blew air under the wheels, causing the plastic sheet that covered the vehicle to inflate in the draught.

I pushed on. With luck I'd find my friends soon.

But life isn't always so kind. A moment later I found scratch marks on a wall. On the floor were the remains of a poster. From what I could make out it had been a picture of a man and a women with children.

Their faces had been clawed away as if some creature hated the sight of humans.

A huge shiver crawled up my spine. So: whatever lurked down here didn't like people. That's a fact. What's more, its claws were so powerful they'd etched deep lines in the concrete wall when it destroyed the poster. I found myself touching my face. What would those claws feel like when they hooked into your skin?

'Keep moving,' I murmured, 'whatever happens, just keep moving. You don't want to be standing here when it comes round that corner.'

10

Leading off from this section of tunnel were rooms. Although deep underground they were dry. They didn't smell bad. Objects lay on tables beneath more plastic covers. Those stretched out forms made me uneasy. Bodies under sheets? Well, that's what they looked like. I made myself check them, otherwise my imagination would riot. I'd find myself picturing zombies rising from their tables of death. When I poked back the covers with a mop I found in a corner I saw that the 'zombie' shapes were only blankets packed in cellophane.

In every room hunched objects in the shadows suggested demon shapes. Elsewhere, were skeletons of mechanical equipment. Computer screens stared – all blank and hollow. Pipes gurgled softly, mocking me. Lights flickered. They seemed to be enjoying the fact I was scared. When they dimmed they seemed to be saying, *Hey, Naz. At any moment we can switch ourselves off. How are you going to get out of here in the dark, Naz? Where will you go? When it's all black and you're scrambling to get out, and your hands touch a face covered in bristly hair, what you gonna do, then?*

I was edgy. Sweat made my back sticky. Nerves

filled my stomach with butterflies. When I came across a door bearing the words: *Gun Store* I was ready to steal a rifle to protect myself. I groaned in disappointment: the gun room was padlocked shut.

With the silence weighing heavy, I rejoined the tunnel. Echoing footsteps – my own. Where were my friends? Were they okay? I passed ten trucks parked nose to tail. Plastic sheets rustled. It was the air-conditioning units that caused the draughts. They made a sinister whispering. The air blew into my back. *Those electric fans are strong,* I thought. Plastic covers rippled. A loose end flew up to catch my ear. *This isn't right. How could fans be* that *strong?*

Like white rats running across the floor, pieces of torn poster scurried. Lights flickered. The breeze got stronger. Plastic flapped with a snapping sound. I tried to ignore the blast of air in my back. Only the fans … nothing to worry about …

Unless …

I stopped dead. I knew I must look back.

Only I daren't.

Because I knew what I'd see. This breeze? It was like being in a subway station when a train rushes through its tunnel to the platform.

The truth struck hard as a punch: *Something's coming this way. Something big. Something fast!*

11

Run? But fleeing will do no good. You can't outrun this.

The breeze became a hurricane. Plastic sheets went crazy. Flapping, snapping, pieces ripped off. They shot down the tunnel like speeding phantoms. Lights dipped. Winked out. Darkness.

Utter darkness.

By touch alone I found one of the trucks. The cover whipped my face. Torrents of ice cold air roared. A charge of menace filled the place. There was the sense of something approaching.

You can't out-run it, I told myself. Gotta hide!

The light flickered on in this section of tunnel. To my left and right, the tunnel was drowned in blackness. I couldn't see a thing there. But I knew the monster charged toward me. Yes! I screamed the word inside my mind: *monster!* It couldn't be anything else but a monster. I'd seen the gouge marks in the steel door. Then those helmets with holes bitten into them. Now – down in this maze of tunnels a monster ran as fast as a train. It was fierce and crazy – and hungry. A blazing hunger for human flesh. Instinct told me the brutal truth.

In three seconds flat I ducked under the plastic,

opened the door to the truck's cab, then hauled myself inside. There I sat behind the huge black ring of the steering wheel. I saw nothing much through the windows, only plastic rippling against glass.

Once again, the light went out. Dark. So dark I couldn't see my own hands. No way would I be crazy enough to switch on the cab light, even if the battery still worked. A light, a movement, just a tiny, little sound from me would tell the monster where I hid. What followed then … good grief, I didn't even want to think about it.

But what did happen then was so strange. For a moment I wondered if I imagined it … so weird … disturbing … unpleasant …

As I sat there in the cab of the truck I tried not to move. All of sudden it went quiet. The blast of air stopped. All those plastic sheets stopped their flapping. I could see nothing … way too dark for that. But from the soft, rustling noise I could picture the truck covers settling back down to hang limp … just like shrouds that cover the deceased. My heart beat with a dull rhythm. Time seemed to stand still. A pain started in my head. A thin, sharp one. A bit like an ice-cream headache. Brain freeze.

Strange.

I tried to rub my head but could hardly lift my arms. Why had I gone so weak? A dizziness made my head droop. All of a sudden I felt half-asleep. My head tilted again. Kinda woozy. My arms were peculiar. Floppy. All strength gone.

At that moment the light returned. Only much dimmer than before. A grey radiance seeped through the plastic. I gazed down almost dreamily at my hands; they sagged limp as dead birds on my legs. The headache got worse. It should have made me wake up, only I became even more drowsy. This was like being in bed and hovering in that floaty borderland between being awake and sleep. I gazed at the dashboard with its big speedometer and rev counter staring back like round eyes.

Then ... a sound ...

With a huge effort I turned my head. I looked out through the door window at the plastic sheet. This time I realised that it was semi-transparent. Through the milky grey material I saw a shape.

A shape that hadn't been there before.

One that moved slowly ... very slowly. I couldn't say how big it was. But it must have been far bigger than a man. Colours were impossible to distinguish. All I could make out were patches of light and dark. It moved slowly. Yet an altogether different aspect of the massive body troubled me more than words could say. And it was this. When the thing stopped moving *there was something on its back that continued to move.* My heart thumped. My blood became ice. Because it was this strange effect that disturbed me most. *Objects were in motion at the top of the shape.* I couldn't see what they were because the plastic wasn't properly transparent. All I could make out were blurred patches. They moved fast. A kind of scrambling motion. Then came a growling voice: 'Neefer-ratt-saaar.'

At that time I could barely move. Dizziness gripped me. A pain still shot through my head.

'You're doing this to me,' I murmured. 'You're affecting my brain. You're causing the pain in my head.' Drowsily, I continued to stare.

In that weird state of mind I didn't worry about being found. At any moment, I expected the plastic to be ripped aside. I'd be face-to-face with this creature. This monster of the labyrinth.

12

But as I sat in the truck, waiting for the monster to lunge through the plastic then drag me, howling, out of the cab, something else happened. Something unexpected. And somehow so worrying that at times I thought the shock would make my heart stop dead.

The pain in my head, the dizziness, the strange attack of exhaustion – I knew the monster did this to me. A sixth-sense inside of me warned that it had the power of mind control. That it could induce paralysis along with the headache and tiredness. Then came something extra. A weird sensation crept into my brain. It arrived in invisible waves from that figure, with the squirming back shapes, at the other side of the plastic cover.

At first I thought it was because I was so drowsy. Yet all of a sudden images flashed through my head. They seemed like fragments of a dream. At the time, I couldn't say for sure if they were dream or not. Or whether the monster fired these pictures into my head.

The weariness grew worse. I could hardly focus my eyes the headache was so painful. But creeping through my skull like cold, menacing phantoms came images – these images were of my friends. Jenny, Pitt,

Adam. Wide-eyed. Anxious faces beneath harsh lights. I grew tense. Maybe it would be like when I imagined the police in those white forensic suits? Only there was something different about this. Although I sat behind the steering wheel in that truck I seemed to be able to see my friends in another part of the tunnel. However, I didn't see all three at once. This wasn't like watching CCTV. *This was seeing through their eyes.* One moment, I looked through Adam's eyes, then Jenny's, then Pitt's. When my vision was channelled through them I caught snatches of their thoughts. Adam's, especially, resonated with fear. Cold, cold terror crept into his heart. *It's not good down here ... bad things happen in these tunnels ... danger ... horror ... people have cried down here ... with loneliness ... fright ... despair ...they were chased ... caught ... hurt ... badly hurt ... I want to go home ...*

Jenny and Pitt were entering a warehouse. Even though they were deep underground the roof must have been nearly twenty feet above them. Lining this cavern of a place were huge steel shelves that filled one wall.

I tried to stop the stream of pictures gushing through my head. Yet this didn't seem like a dream, or imagination. By some telepathic power I knew I was seeing what they were *really* doing ... and through their eyes. But what if it turned bad? Really, really bad? My heart lurched as I imagined their fate.

With all my will power I tried to snap out of this trance, but I couldn't. What's more, I couldn't move a muscle. All I could do was sit there, frozen. Using all my strength, I managed to turn my eyes to where the creature stood. At that moment it moved away. The plastic blurred everything. Far too blurred to make out any detail. Yet I saw squirming objects appear to ride on its back. Call it intuition, but I sensed the creature had noticed something that needed a closer look. Then I slipped into that trance again. With an uncanny clarity my friends' actions were recorded by my mind's eye. Their thoughts pierced my nerves. Deep down I knew exactly where the monster was headed. Worse, I couldn't do a thing to warn the three. This is what I saw inside my head – and through their eyes:

'How do they reach the ones higher up?' Adam asked. He was staring at the shelves. But his thoughts clamoured: *Want to go home ... Not good here. Something might hurt us ...*

'See those ladders set on runners?' Jenny pointed. 'They can be rolled to wherever they're needed.'

Pitt said, 'I'm not bothered about shelves full of boxes. Where's Naz?'

Adam shivered. 'First, where's the exit? Remember that thing we saw?'

'Did anyone see what it looked like?' Jenny asked.

Pitt shrugged. 'Too far away. Just a speck in the distance.'

Adam said. 'But you could tell it was huge. It nearly filled the tunnel.'

'And it was fast,' Jenny added.

Pitt looked back. Tunnel lights gleamed on vehicle shrouds.

Jenny's eyes widened. 'What's wrong. Pitt? What have you seen?'

'Naz?' asked Adam, hopefully.

'It's not a person. Too big.' He suddenly hissed. 'It's coming this way.'

Jenny whirled round. 'Hide on the shelves. Get right behind the boxes.'

Adam groaned. 'It's bound to find us.'

'Once you've found somewhere keep absolutely

still. Don't make a noise.'

The lights flickered. A breeze blew along the tunnel. Discarded pieces of paper and old gum wrappers slithered along the floor. They knew *it* raced toward them.

Quickly, the three found their hiding places. Jenny climbed the ladder up fifteen feet to a shelf full of packed rice. There, she hunkered down behind dozens of boxes. Pitt hauled himself up to a shelf as high as his head. Engine parts, dozens of them, all wrapped in polythene. For some reason they made him think of human skulls in polythene bags. Adam went low. He wriggled under the bottom shelf then lay with his back on the concrete floor. Its coldness seeped through his clothes to touch his skin. The steel panel of the shelf was just two inches above him. He remembered how crabs lodged themselves into gaps between boulders on the seashore. For him this seemed the safest place.

A moment later the light died away until it was so dim Jenny could only make out indistinct box-shapes on the shelf. She winced. A pain flared up over her eye. Like when you drink ice-cold milk too fast.

On the shelf just at head height Pitt lay still. Then he realised that it wasn't will-power keeping him immobile. He found it hard to move. A strange paralysis gripped him. When he heard the pad of feet in the tunnel he tried to shuffle even closer to the wall for protection. But he couldn't lift his arm never mind move his body.

On the floor under the bottom shelf Adam found even moaning beyond him when the pain started in his forehead. His strength vanished. It was all he could do to turn his head to one side. When he did a dizzy, woozy sensation made him feel as if he was falling over the edge of the cliff. The moment he closed his eyes the vertigo grew even worse. *I hope it doesn't see us ... if it does it will hurt us ... blood will be shed ...*

All Adam could do was lie there as some enormous form entered the tunnel.

13

Peeping through gaps on the shelves, Pitt and Jenny tried to see what had arrived in this gloomy cavern. There was no doubting the beast's size. Even from his hiding place on the floor, Adam looked, too. But all three felt strangely dizzy. Their limbs didn't work properly. They felt sleepy. And all three had the same sharp pain boring through their skulls. This is how they stayed for the next thirty seconds. Then, as if the beast, had satisfied itself that there was nothing of interest in this area, it padded away.

When they felt that it was safe to emerge they crept from their hiding places. All three agreed amongst themselves how ill they'd felt. All of them noticed how the light had dimmed when the creature had entered this section of tunnel. But when they all tried to describe what they had seen of the beast no single one could agree on a description.

Adam declared, 'I could see paws. Four of them. Like a lion's.'

Jenny disagreed. 'A lion? It was nothing like a lion. When I looked down at it from above I could see tentacles. Masses of tentacles. They were bright green.'

Pitt shook his head. 'From where I was I could see bare skin, maybe its belly ... there's no fur, and certainly no tentacles. There were mottled patches on its body. I saw that kind of pattern once on something in a reptile house at the zoo.'

'I had the best view,' Jenny declared. 'From right up there. It's like a giant octopus.'

'No way an octopus,' Pitt insisted. 'It's a gargantuan lizard.'

'You're both wrong,' Adam told them. 'It's a mammal. I saw furry paws. Probably a specially bred attack lion.'

'Attack lion,' Pitt snorted. 'You'll have had your eyes shut anyway.'

'Are you calling me a coward?'

It was a dangerous thing to do. But for the moment they forgot about the real possibility the creature might come back. Instead, they bickered over what they did or didn't see.

14

At the same time as the trio argued I was still in the truck. Five minutes ago, the monster had left my section of tunnel. Immediately the pain in my head went, too. But for those five minutes I was held in that trance. By some telepathic force I'd seen what was happening to Jenny, Pitt and Adam. What's more, I knew what they had felt and thought. Somehow the creature had been responsible for that effect. Fortunately, as the minutes passed, and that thing moved further from me, I felt better. The light grew brighter. The dizziness vanished. I could move my arms normally again. The moment my legs worked as they should I climbed out of the cab, ready to search for my three friends.

When I turned a corner I started to find some answers. The next tunnel was different. Instead of bare concrete walls they were covered with white tiles. Kind of clinical. Here there weren't any trucks under plastic sheets. Instead, four red cylinders in a row. Each as big as a car. They lay on their sides on V shaped racks. Odd … very odd.

These were troubling to look at. They resembled the thing you might see towed behind a farm tractor, but they were covered in warnings. *CAUTION: LIQUID NITROGEN INLET. BEWARE: SUB-ZERO TEMPERATURE.* Worst of all: *DO NOT TOUCH: DANGEROUS CONTENT.* I shuddered. Were these nuclear weapons? I walked along the line of cylinders. Stencilled on each one, in fierce, spiky letters was: *VOGGRON.* And after that mystifying word, either an A or B or C or a D. So the first cylinder was labelled *VOGGRON A.*

When I reached *VOGGRON C* I groaned, 'Oh, no.'

The third cylinder had been bashed hard. Dents covered it. Only the dents bulged outward not inward. One end of the cylinder had been torn away. The metal cap, which was six feet in diameter, lay on the tiled floor. The cylinder itself was clean inside. Completely empty.

VOGGRON. Now I knew what had smashed open the bunker door. What's more, I knew EXACTLY what had chased us. As I stood there, a darkness fell over me. It spilled across the floor, growing bigger as some shape – one that cast a long, dark shadow – crept up behind me.

Even though I wanted to move I couldn't. Like one of those dreams when you need to run but can't move so much as a finger. Then came its touch on my shoulder.

'Hey, Naz, what you found here?'

'*Jenny?*' I spun round. 'Adam? Pitt? I thought it had got you.'

'We thought it was *you* who'd been nabbed.'

Grimly, I said, 'If we don't get out of here fast we're all done for.' I nodded at the cylinder. 'By what was in there. The Voggron.'

Adam saw the wrecked cylinder. 'It broke out of that tank, didn't it? It escaped from the bunker, now it's back.'

I frowned. 'But why would it come back?'

Pitt rubbed his jaw. 'Maybe the Voggron doesn't like being outdoors. Or it needs to return to its lair.'

'But what is it?' Jenny examined the cylinders.

I shrugged. 'Earlier, I hid in a truck when it came along the tunnel. I didn't see it exactly ...'

'I did,' Jenny said. It's got masses of tentacles. Like a giant octopus.'

'Don't listen to her,' Pitt grunted. 'I saw it. It's a big lizard.'

'You didn't see all of it.' Jenny got angry. 'I was fifteen feet up on a shelf. I saw tentacles, round suckers, green skin, the works.'

'No, no.' Adam seemed to pity them. 'I was closest. I saw paws. With fur. The Voggron's more like a lion.'

Jenny turned to me. 'Naz, tell them what you saw.'

'It's weird. I saw ...' Yes! I had seen through their eyes. A kind of telepathy had been at work. I wanted to tell them all about it. How I'd known their thoughts. *But what if they think I'm crazy?* Suddenly, telling them everything didn't seem a good idea. At least not at that moment. Instead, I gave a baffled shrug. 'The truck was covered in plastic. All I did see was a figure ... just blurred through the sheet.' But I now knew what those squirming shapes were on its back. Tentacles. Just the thought of them made my own back itch.

'So ...' Jenny slapped her forehead in exasperation. 'We all saw it, but we all saw something different.'

'A lizard,' Pitt insisted.

Adam shook his head. 'Big cat. Lion, maybe.'

I held up one hand. 'But we can all agree that it came out of there.' I tapped the empty cylinder with my knuckles. It made a gong sound that echoed away into the distance. A ghostly shimmer on the cold air.

'And there's another thing.' Jenny was deadly serious. 'Although we can't agree on what we saw, we can agree on how we felt.'

Adam pointed to his forehead. 'A headache. The worst I've had.'

We all nodded.

'Like an ice cream headache, only multiplied a hundred times.' Jenny rubbed the back of her neck as if it still ached. 'And all the strength went out of me.'

I shuddered. 'I don't know if it was my eyes, or the power supply, but it went dark.'

Pitt became uneasy, too. 'And when it came close, and the headache started, and you felt like crud, wasn't that the moment that you didn't care whether it found you or not?'

I agreed. 'The Voggron did that to us. It can mess with our minds.' Again, I nearly told them that, just for a few moment, I'd been able to see through their eyes. But I decided to wait until one of them mentioned it. I didn't want them to think I'd gone nuts. So, I just added vaguely, 'Brain control. It's a psychic transmitter.'

'That's impossible,' Jenny said. But from her expression you could tell she knew it was the truth. The Voggron had telepathic powers. Even so, she didn't know the half of its unnatural talents.

'Think about it,' said Pitt. 'Wouldn't that be the perfect weapon? One that makes the enemy too sick and too weak to fight. Not only that, it can reach into your head and stop you even wanting to save your own life.'

And it can make you see through other people's eyes. *Why didn't these three experience the same thing?* I wondered. *Why me ... have I got something in common with the Voggron?*

'A secret weapon,' Adam sounded panicky. 'A

Frankenstein soldier.'

'But it didn't know we were there,' Jenny protested, 'so how could it reprogram our brains?'

I stared at the cylinder. 'It does it all the time, but only over a short range. And it's only temporary. Otherwise it would affect those on its own side.'

Pitt whistled. 'So the Voggron is a weapon. Just like the guns stored down here.'

'Whatever it looks like,' Jenny added, 'it was kept frozen. When they needed it to fight the enemy it would be thawed out.'

'Only it's defrosted too soon. Maybe a circuit blew.' Pitt whistled again. 'That means there's three more in these.' He tapped an intact cylinder with his knuckles. Instantly a loud bang filled the vault. A sound like thunder. His eyes went wide. 'Something just hit the cylinder wall from inside.'

Adam gulped. 'It's wanting to break out, too. Guys, we gotta find the exit.'

Pitt backed away from the cylinder as a rumbling came from it. 'We could try going back to the lounge.'

In a very quiet voice, Jenny whispered, 'Too late. It's already here.'

15

There are times you think your eyes are cheating you. It must be imagination, you tell yourself. Or I'm not seeing properly, or it's a dream. Only when I backed away I clunked into the wall. It hurt enough to prove this was no dream. Picture this: An animal that's bigger than an adult lion. The creature prowls into the tunnel. It has a massive head with two fiery orange eyes, big jaws and a mane. Apart from the mane, and tufts of hair on its paws, it has no fur. The skin is yellow with blood-red patches. Pitt was right, it does resemble the skin of a lizard. It walks on all fours. From its back swarm green tentacles. At least fifty of them, like the tentacles of an octopus. These don't sag but writhe in the air. They move with a quick, muscular strength. Each one is perhaps ten feet long. They reach out to touch objects: the light fittings, the cable ducts, the plumbing pipes. It must be using a refined sense of touch to map its environment. That and its eyes and other senses must create a perfect understanding of where it is. And it's not just how monstrous the Voggron looks, it's that nasty trick it can do – to hurt you without even touching. The headache started in my head. My shoulders sagged as the strength seeped from my body. All of a sudden I found it hard to stand on my own two feet.

Despite his fear, Pitt was in awe. 'Folks. Meet the Voggron.'

Adam gaped. 'Earlier we all saw *parts* of it. Me, paws. Jenny, tentacles ...'

Jenny shouted, 'RUN!'

The lion-like creature, with octopus tentacles writhing from its back, leapt forward. Its jaws opened wide to reveal huge teeth, sharp as steak knives. Slashing behind it, a long bullwhip of a tail. It lashed this flailing appendage in our direction. In absolute horror I saw that the tail ended in claws. Huge curving claws. The tail slammed into the wall above my head. Its wicked claws raked the tiles. As I ducked I saw the gouge marks. If that whip-tail had hit me in the face? Think of the savage cuts!

We all ran in different directions. It followed me at first. Its paws thumped the floor, then, when I ducked under a low doorway to a storeroom, it changed direction to race after Adam. At the same time one tentacle on its back snapped out to curl round Jenny's waist. With an uncanny dexterity it gripped the back of her jacket. As it did that, it let fly with the whip-tail again. It struck a steel girder next to Pitt. Sparks flew.

Jenny was in deep trouble. It didn't loosen its grip on her fabric. Quickly, it dragged the girl toward its huge mouth filled with champing teeth. Then it happened again. I found myself looking through Jenny's eyes into the monster's hate-filled face. The orange eyes blazed. Closer ... and closer. The mouth opened. In total shock I yelled. A yell so loud that the Voggron glanced back for the source of the noise. Jenny took her chance; she slipped out of the jacket, leaving it swinging in the tentacle's grasp, then she hid behind a row of water pipes.

Deciding to attack Adam from above, the beast chose to leap onto one of the cylinders but misjudged its landing. It slipped off the curving metal to fall into the narrow gap at the other side. Frantically, it struggled to free itself. Even so, it bellowed in fury. I could see tentacles whipping the air before they latched onto the cylinder. Once it had a grip it could begin to heave itself out. For a second I watched those thick, rubbery limbs in fascination. Suckers gripped the cylinder. I felt its effect on my mind grow stronger – the headache, the weakness. Lights grew dim. Jenny pushed me.

'Come on! Now's our chance to get back to the exit.'

Boy, how we ran! Summoning what was left of our strength, we belted along the tunnel lined with vehicles. Once we'd got some distance between us and the Voggron the ill-effects inflicted by its wicked telepathic power faded. The light grew brighter. Strength returned to our legs.

'It's coming!' I yelled.

Adam gasped, 'We'll never make it.'

'Adam, run!'

'We're going to die down here.'

'Keep moving. Get up those steps.'

I was the last one to the stairwell that led up to the lounge. Quickly, I glanced back along that long corridor. In the distance I saw a yellow object. At first, just a little yellow blob. But it got bigger and bigger the closer it got. And that monster moved FAST. It soon became clear it was the creature from the cylinder store. The mane, the yellow body with red patches, the tentacles, the whip-tail with claws. *Here it comes ... the Voggron ... legs pounding, jaws open wide. If those tentacles should grip your head? Slimy, wet suckers. And just imagine its teeth sinking into your throat.* Taking a deep breath, I followed the other three as they clattered up the steps.

I shouted, 'I figure we've got fifteen seconds before that thing reaches us.'

With a cry Adam collapsed. 'I can't run any further. I've got a stitch.'

All three of us grabbed him by the arms, then heaved him to his feet.

'Keep moving,' Jenny urged. 'We'll lock the lounge door. It won't be able to follow us.'

When we reached the living quarters door I groaned with disappointment. 'The lock's broken. It must have done it when it escaped.'

'What now?'

I shouted, 'It's coming up the stairs! We won't reach the exit in time.' Heavy paws thumped. 'Scatter … hide … anywhere.'

'It's no good,' Adam groaned. 'It'll find us.'

Yet fear drove us to find hiding places. We ran by sofas, looking for rooms to lock ourselves in. Only they had flimsy doors that the monster could shred in seconds.

Adam curled under the kitchen table. 'We're going to be eaten alive!'

I raced by the big TV screen – if only that six foot wide square of glass was a doorway to the outside world! An onscreen message read, *GAME PAUSED*.

Then – BANG! The door shattered. The Voggron flicked aside what panels remained as if they were shreds of paper. Then it prowled into the lounge with all the menace of a hungry lion. Its tentacles curled in the air. Then a strange thing happened. The tentacles darted out to open cupboard doors, so it could check inside. Maybe it thought we'd hidden in them? And it was all so fast. Flick, flick – glance, glance. Those strange words it had used before came in a soft growl, *'Neefer-ratt-saaar.'* The whip-tail came up as if to stroke the ceiling. Despite, the tail moving only slowly its formidable tail claws scratched deep groves into the plasterwork. It took pleasure in the action. An orange lip curled back in a weird smile. Sharp fangs glinted.

Remember, its hatred for humans? That shredded poster? And didn't I sense its raging hunger? That it longed to sink its teeth into a fresh, living body.

So what are we? Snacks on legs?

Jenny hid behind a sofa. I ducked into a space between the kitchen sink and a dishwasher. Adam stayed under his table. Pitt stood with his back to the wall beside the giant TV screen.

All useless hiding places. The Voggron moved with fluid grace across the room.

As it approached, the headaches started. My legs turned wobbly. Pitt's eyes became dull as if he'd fall asleep. And the blood-thirsty Voggron came ever closer … and closer.

Despite the pain in my head, and the way the monster could affect my eyes so it seemed to be growing suddenly darker, I forced myself to watch it. And I could tell it was vicious. Even the faint hum of the refrigerator enraged it. With one of its front paws it struck out. Easily, it ripped away the fridge door. Then it swept all those chocolate bars out over the carpet. The ketchup bottle cracked open. Sauce splashed out onto the carpet like blood had been spilt.

Soon real blood will be splattering the floor.

The Voggron saw Pitt standing by the TV. Those

ravenous orange eyes fixed on his face. He froze, not daring to move. It took a step nearer. Sniffed the air. Then it took another step toward him. When he flinched it opened its jaws. Fangs glistened. Tentacles danced in the air. A snarl began in its throat. The weird mind effect kicked in. I caught glimpses of what Pitt was seeing. I saw through his eyes. I felt his fear. And all the time the monster's face grew larger and larger the closer it got.

Jenny jumped up. 'Naz! The remote control's on the table. Grab it!'

I stared at her like she'd gone mad.

'You're the closest,' she hissed. 'Quick, before it attacks Pitt.'

For some reason I grabbed the remote control but I didn't know what good it would do. I could hardly thump the monster with it, could I? It wouldn't even bruise its yellow lizard skin. Also, I was so dizzy by this time. The headache blurred my vision. Once again it happened. For a split second I saw through Jenny's eyes. I saw ME standing there with the remote control hanging limply in my hand. My eyes were dull … as blank as dead TV screens … as if my mind had been disconnected from my body. *Naz is in shutdown. He's gone zombie …*

Snarling, the Voggron moved closer to Pitt. The boy stared death in the eye.

Jenny hissed, 'Naz. Hit *Resume Play.*'

'Why?' Her demand baffled me. Everything seemed hazy. Far away.

'Remember, it's a war game. The Voggron's meant to fight enemy soldiers. You might be able to distract it long enough to –'

The yellow monster took another step toward Pitt. Now only ten feet separated them. It tensed itself, ready to attack. The remote control felt as heavy as concrete in my hand. If it slipped from my fingers I'd be too far gone to pick it up again. My head throbbed ... everything just so woozy ... dream-like.

'Naz!' Jenny shouted. 'You've got to press the button.'

I stared. My head hurt. All the strength had gone from my fingers.

Jenny pleaded, 'Naz, you're Pitt's only chance. HE'S GOING TO DIE!'

Pitt, die? No! How I managed I don't know. *Bosh!* I hit *Resume Play.* Instantly a silver android appeared on screen. It raced forward as if about to run from the TV. Bigger and bigger. In a second the android nearly filled the screen. It had long silver legs and steel body armour. The Voggron reacted instantly. It turned its attention from Pitt to the menacing android. But did it realise it was only a computer game? Did it really fear the silver warrior could hurt it?

'Run, Pitt, run!'

The Voggron roared. Its claws ripped furrows in the carpet. The whip-tail lashed. Ceiling lamps shattered. Before it could lose interest in the TV I hit the *Fire* button. Purple flame shot from the android's blaster.

The next second the Voggron attacked the screen. Glass exploded. Claws ripped at cables. High voltage in the electronics zapped it hard. Tentacles yanked out circuit boards. Flashes. Smoke. Sparks. Then it bit the mother-board. *Bang!* The TV exploded. The Voggron's snarl became a scream. All of a sudden it dropped down to the floor. There it lay. Not a sound came from it. Tentacles flopped down limp. Instantly, we felt okay again. The headache and exhaustion vanished.

Adam was amazed. 'You've killed it.'

Cautiously, I took a closer look at the dead monster. 'It will have been made in a laboratory. It was never even properly alive.'

Jenny headed for the exit. 'Time to leave, guys.'

Soon we were out in the fresh air. The hot sun shone like it was the birth of a new world. Its brilliance dazzled us. We headed across the grass toward the hole in the fence. The quicker we were away from the bunker the better.

At that moment a motorbike roared up. The rider stopped the machine next to us and then grinned at Pitt. He especially took notice of the cut on his mouth.

'How's the lip, Pitt?'

'Brian, we don't want any trouble.' Pitt shook his head, exhausted. 'We've had more than enough already today.'

'Oooh, the lip still looks sore. Did Momma put some creamy-weamy on it for you?'

Pitt leapt at Brian. For a moment Brian was astonished that this boy, who was a lot smaller than him, had decided to attack. Pitt dragged him off the motorbike as an object seemed to drop from the sky.

'It's the Voggron,' Jenny shouted. 'The electric shock only stunned it!'

Brian scrambled away in terror. Pitt ran, too. We fled into the bushes. The Voggron directed its fury at the motorbike. The noisy motor angered it. The monster ripped away the seat with its claws, then it bit big black chunks out of the tyres. Meanwhile, its green tentacles tore the brakes and handlebars into little pieces.

For a moment the engine raced out of control. The noise was so loud it made the creature even more furious. It reared up on its hind legs then smashed down with both front paws onto the bike. The crushed remains blew out a jet of oily smoke then the motor stopped dead.

Brian's voice was croaky with fear. 'What is that thing?'

'The Voggron,' Adam told him.

'Where did it come from?'

Pitt looked grim. 'Never mind where it came from, the problem is what it's going to do to us now?'

Brian sagged to his knees. Either through fear or the telepathic effect from the monster.

Jenny called out, 'It's up to us, guys. No-one else can save us. We've got find a way to fight that thing.'

'How?' Adam swallowed.

'We use our brains. There's a way to figure this out.'

'Jenny's right,' Pitt said. 'It doesn't like noise. Look how it's taking that motorbike apart. It's making sure it never works again.'

'Which gives us a few seconds to come up with an answer.' Jenny glanced from face to face. 'Apart from noise, what else doesn't it like?'

'Us,' Adam whispered.

'What else?'

'Think quickly,' I said. 'It's starting to lose interest in the bike.'

Pitt stared at the bunker door. 'It took a lot of trouble to break out of there, but then it went back into the tunnels. Why?'

This time Adam came up with an answer. 'It doesn't like being outdoors.'

'Why?'

We all looked up at the brilliant sun shining down. This June day was going to be a hot one. The light seared our eyes.

We all shouted at the same time. *'Sunlight!'*

I peered from the bushes at the snarling Voggron. 'Look at that thing, guys. What's happening to it?'

Out there on the grass by the shattered motorbike the Voggron grunted. It shook its head as if angry at something we couldn't see.

All of us, apart from Brian, who was frozen in fear, studied the creature.

'Something's different.' Adam frowned.

'What's wrong with its skin?'

'It wasn't like that before. It's changing colour.'

Jenny added triumphantly, 'Sunburn!'

She spoke too loudly because the Voggron realised we were in the bushes. It took a lurching step toward us. The tail whipped angrily.

But I realised something else now. Yes, the once yellow skin had turned to a sore-looking red. And as for its eyes?

I hissed. 'It's eyes were orange. Now they're white.'

Pitt whooped. 'The sun's hurting its eyes. It can't see properly.'

'But it can hear us,' Adam groaned. 'It's coming this way.'

It darted toward the bushes. The tentacles reached out to feel the branch of a tree. Even though it couldn't see much, it could hear … and with those tentacles it could feel. And there was nothing wrong with its sharp teeth or that whip-tail with the claws. If it grabbed us that would be it. Dead meat.

'Spread out,' Jenny said. 'Then start calling.'

We did as she said.

After running to different parts of the fenced compound we all started yelling out loud. All apart from

Brian, that is; he curled up under a bush and whimpered.

We shouted:

'Here.'

'No, over here!'

'Come and get me!'

'Yahoo!'

Those shouts from all different directions confused the Voggron. Disorientated it. The beast whirled round. Sometimes it attacked a bush with its teeth, or whipped a tree trunk with its clawed tail. Splinters flew.

Jenny hollered, 'It can't find us! Keep shouting.'

The creature's skin turned crimson. Its eyes were pure white now. Blind ... sightless ... But the monster's fury increased.

'We can't keep shouting forever,' I called out. 'Pitt! Help me with this.'

I grabbed at the sign bolted to the fence. It bore the stark warning:

CAUTION!
RESTRICTED MILITARY ZONE
DO NOT PASS.
DANGER OF DEATH!

This was the same sign that Pitt thumped angrily before we entered the bunker. The danger notice had been printed on a big metal sheet, then fixed to a wooden backing. After all these years the metal had started to peel away. Pitt didn't know what I'd figured out but he helped me pull the steel sheet away from the timber board. Although the screws had rusted away, making it come free easily, it was almost the size of house door: so awkwardly cumbersome that it needed both of us, working together, to carry it. Then trouble. The metal sheet was bendy. When it wobbled it made a loud metallic *Wub-Wub-Wub.* The noise alerted the Voggron. It turned menacingly to the source of the clanking.

Snarling, the monster took a step toward us.

'This better be good,' Pitt said, 'because in five seconds that thing's going to chew us to mush.'

'Turn the sign round,' I told him.

When he saw the other side of the danger sign was bare, silvery metal – as bright as a mirror – he whooped. 'Bingo! Naz, you're a genius!'

The Voggron homed in on our voices. It ran across the grass. Jaws opened wide. Teeth! So many, sharp murderous teeth.

Then – whoosh.

We used the metal sheet like a giant reflector. Sunlight bounced off of it into the face of the Voggron. It must have known that it had been blasted by an even brighter light than the June sunshine because with a roar it stopped running toward us. Then, like a dog chasing its own tail, it began to spin. Round and round. Faster and faster. It spun until the green tentacles, mane, whip-tail, and red body became a blur of colours. What happened next caught us all by surprise.

The colours vanished. They were replaced by black … deep, deep black.

'It's gone,' Pitt uttered in amazement.

'Keep the light on it,' I told him. 'We've got to be sure.' So we held the metal sheet so it reflected intense, blinding sunlight on the monster. Seconds later I realised that the spinning blackness was a swirling dust cloud. Just black particles. A twister made from dark grains.

'Okay, we can stop now.' We let the danger sign

fall down into the grass. After that we all gathered round where the monster had done its last mad dance. All that remained of the Voggron was a pile of black dust.

Jenny heaved a sigh of relief. 'The sunlight you reflected onto the creature killed it.'

'Like I said,' I managed a smile, 'I don't think it was ever alive. Not properly anyway.' At that moment, I realised my smile was a false one. Because a sudden doubt smacked into me. Listen, the Voggron affected me in a way that was completely different to what the other three experienced. Briefly, I'd seen through their eyes, knew their thoughts, felt what they were feeling. Why me? What made me different to them? Had the Voggron infected me in some way? Or did it go further back than today? Am I different to them because of what happened when I was younger?

The truth is, I'm adopted. The man and woman who became my parents found me in a cardboard box when I was baby. That box had been in the lane just outside the bunker fence. Both tell me they remember that night well. The moon shone bright.

And for the first time in their lives they'd seen that the bunker door was open. Wide open. A ghostly blue light shone inside. In the morning the steel door was locked shut again.

The shiver that ran up my spine made my back itch. A squirmy itch that made the skin on my back so sensitive I couldn't bear the pressure of even my T-shirt against it. If anyone else noticed I was troubled they didn't mention it.

Adam looked into the distance. 'Army helicopters. See? Four of them. They must have received an alarm call from computers in the bunker.'

With an effort I made that false smile on my face

even bigger. 'We'll leave the experts to clear up the mess.'

Jenny noticed Brian still gawped in shock at the wreckage of his bike. Before we headed home, she said to Pitt. 'You saved Brian's life.' She grinned. 'Something tells me he's never going to even think of bullying you again. *Ever.*'

They were laughing with relief that the danger was over. I laughed, too, though I found myself thinking hard about the Voggron. For a while back there in the tunnels, my mind had evolved into an uncannily powerful instrument. One that could reach into other people's minds – just as the Voggron had done. When my back gave that itchy squirm again I asked myself the question:

Is this story really over?

Or, for me, had it only just begun?

Other Telos Titles Available

URBAN GOTHIC: LACUNA AND OTHER TRIPS
edited by DAVID J HOWE
Tales of horror from and inspired by the *Urban Gothic* televison series. Contributors: Graham Masterton, Christopher Fowler, Simon Clark, Steve Lockley & Paul Lewis, Paul Finch and Debbie Bennett.
£8.00 (+ £2.50 UK p&p)
Standard p/b ISBN: 1-903889-00-6

KING OF ALL THE DEAD
by STEVE LOCKLEY & PAUL LEWIS
The king of all the dead will have what is his.
£8.00 (+ £2.50 UK p&p)
Standard p/b ISBN: 1-903889-61-8

THE HUMAN ABSTRACT by GEORGE MANN
A future tale of private detectives, AIs, Nanobots, love and death.
£7.99 (+ £2.50 UK p&p)
Standard p/b ISBN: 1-903889-65-0

BREATHE by CHRISTOPHER FOWLER
The Office meets *Night of the Living Dead*.
£25.00 (+ £2.50 UK p&p)
Deluxe signed and numbered h/b ISBN: 1-903889-68-5

HOUDINI'S LAST ILLUSION by STEVE SAVILE
Can the master illusionist Harry Houdini outwit the dead shades of his past?
£7.99 (+ £2.50 UK p&p)
Standard p/b ISBN: 1-903889-66-9

ALICE'S JOURNEY BEYOND THE MOON
by R J CARTER
A sequel to the classic Lewis Carroll tales.
£6.99 (+ £2.50 UK p&p)
Standard p/b ISBN: 1-903889-76-6
£30.00 (+ £2.50 UK p&p)
Deluxe signed and numbered h/b ISBN: 1-903889-77-4

APPROACHING OMEGA by ERIC BROWN
A colonisation mission to Earth runs into problems.
£7.99 (+ £2.50 UK p&p)
Standard p/b ISBN: 1-903889-98-7
£30.00 (+ £2.50 UK p&p)
Deluxe signed and numbered h/b ISBN: 1-903889-99-5

VALLEY OF LIGHTS by STEPHEN GALLAGHER
A cop comes up against a body-hopping murderer.
£9.99 (+ £3.00 UK p&p)
Standard p/b ISBN: 1-903889-74-X
£30.00 (+ £3.00 UK p&p)
Deluxe signed and numbered h/b ISBN: 1-903889-75-8

PRETTY YOUNG THINGS by DOMINIC MCDONAGH
A nest of lesbian rave bunny vampires is at large in Manchester. When Chelsey's ex-boyfriend is taken as food, Chelsey has to get out fast.
£7.99 (+ £2.50 UK p&p)
Standard p/b ISBN: 1-84583-045-8

A MANHATTAN GHOST STORY by T M WRIGHT
Do you see ghosts? A classic tale of love and the supernatural.
£9.99 (+ £3.00 UK p&p)
Standard p/b ISBN: 1-84583-048-2

SHROUDED BY DARKNESS: TALES OF TERROR
edited by ALISON L R DAVIES
An anthology of tales guaranteed to bring a chill to the spine. This collection has been published to raise money for DebRA, a charity working on behalf of people with the genetic skin blistering condition, Epidermolysis Bullosa. Featuring stories by: Debbie Bennett, Poppy Z Brite, Simon Clark, Storm Constantine, Peter Crowther, Alison L R Davies, Paul Finch, Christopher Fowler, Neil Gaiman, Gary Greenwood, David J Howe, Dawn Knox, Tim Lebbon, Charles de Lint, Steven Lockley & Paul Lewis, James Lovegrove, Graham Masterton, Richard Christian Matheson, Justina Robson, Mark Samuels, Darren Shan and Michael Marshall Smith. With a frontispiece by Clive Barker and a foreword by Stephen Jones. Deluxe hardback cover by Simon Marsden.
£12.99 (+ £3.00 UK p&p)
Standard p/b ISBN: 1-84583-046-6
£50.00 (+ £3.00 UK p&p)
Deluxe signed and numbered h/b ISBN: 978-1-84583-047-2

BLACK TIDE by DEL STONE JR
A college professor and his students find themselves
trapped by an encroaching horde of zombies following a
waste spillage.
£7.99 (+ £2.50 UK p&p)
Standard p/b ISBN: 978-1-84583-043-4

FORCE MAJEURE by DANIEL O'MAHONY
An incredible fantasy novel. Kay finds herself trapped in
a strange city in the Andes … a place where dreams can
become reality, and where dragons may reside.
£7.99 (+ £2.50 UK p&p)
Standard p/b ISBN: 978-1-84583-050-2

THE DJINN by GRAHAM MASTERTON
Graham Masterton's terrifying 1977 novel is republished
by Telos in a brand new edition, complete with an
exclusive introduction by the author.
£9.99 (+ £2.50 UK p&p)
Standard p/b ISBN: 978-1-84583-052-6

RULES OF DUEL by GRAHAM MASTERTON and
WILLIAM S BURROUGHS
A clever and pervasive novel, which turns literature on
its head, and makes the reader work to be part of the
evolving plot. Complete with original introduction by
Burroughs, written before his death in 1997, RULES OF
DUEL is a previously unpublished masterpiece from two
of the greatest writers of their generations.
£9.99 (+ £2.50 UK p&p)
Standard p/b ISBN: 978-1-84583-054-0

ZOMBIES IN NEW YORK AND OTHER BLOODY
JOTTINGS by SAM STONE
Thirteen stories of horror and passion, and six
mythological and erotic poems from the pen of the new
Queen of Vampire fiction.
£12.99 (+ £2.50 UK p&p)
Standard p/b ISBN: 978-1-84583-055-7

TALESPINNING by DAVID J HOWE
Encompassing short stories, screenplays, and extracts
from other pieces, *talespinning* is a fascinating dip into
the unknown. If vampires, imaginary dogs, time-
travelling ghosts and wishes that come true appeal, then
this collection has something for you!
£12.99 (+ £2.50 UK p&p)
Standard p/b ISBN: 978-1-84583-058-8

ZOMBIES AT TIFFANY'S by SAM STONE
A steampunked story of diamonds, chutzpah, death and
horror from the blood-drenched pen of Sam Stone.
£9.99 (+ £2.50 UK p&p)
Standard p/b ISBN 978-1-84583-072-4

The prices shown are correct at time of going to press. However, the publishers reserve the right to increase prices from those previously advertised without prior notice.

TELOS PUBLISHING
c/o Beech House, Chapel Lane, Moulton, Cheshire,
CW9 8PQ, England
Email: orders@telos.co.uk
Web: www.telos.co.uk

To order copies of any Telos books, please visit our website where there are full details of all titles and facilities for worldwide credit card online ordering, as well as occasional special offers, or send a cheque or postal order (UK only) for the appropriate amount (including postage and packing – note that four or more titles are post free in the UK), together with details of the book(s) you require, plus your name and address to the above address. Overseas readers please send two international reply coupons for details of prices and postage rates.

61503159R00116

Made in the USA
Charleston, SC
23 September 2016